Too Many Aliens

DON'T MISS THE REST OF THE
SIXTH-GRADE ALIEN SERIES!

Sixth-Grade Alien
I Shrank My Teacher
Missing — One Brain!
Lunch Swap Disaster
Zombies of the Science Fair
Class Pet Catastrophe
Too Many Aliens

Coming Soon: *Snatched from Earth*

Sixth-Grade Alien

Too Many Aliens

By BRUCE COVILLE

Illustrated by Glen Mullaly

ALADDIN

NEW YORK LONDON TORONTO SYDNEY NEW DELHI

ALADDIN

An imprint of Simon & Schuster Children's Publishing Division

1230 Avenue of the Americas, New York, New York 10020

This Aladdin paperback edition July 2021

Text copyright © 2000, 2021 by Bruce Coville

Illustrations copyright © 2021 by Glen Mullaly

Also available in an Aladdin hardcover edition.

All rights reserved, including the right of reproduction in whole or in part in any form.

ALADDIN and related logo are registered trademarks of Simon & Schuster, Inc.

For information about special discounts for bulk purchases, please contact Simon & Schuster Special Sales at 1-866-506-1949 or business@simonandschuster.com.

The Simon & Schuster Speakers Bureau can bring authors to your live event. For more information or to book an event contact the Simon & Schuster Speakers Bureau at 1-866-248-3049 or visit our website at www.simonspeakers.com.

Book designed by Tiara Iandiorio

The illustrations for this book were rendered in a mix of traditional and digital media.

The text of this book was set in Noyh Book.

Manufactured in the United States of America 0621 OFF

2 4 6 8 10 9 7 5 3 1

Library of Congress Control Number 2020952029

ISBN 9781534487253 (hc)

ISBN 9781534487246 (pbk)

ISBN 9781534487260 (ebook)

FOR TONY SANSEVERO,
EXCELLENT FRIEND AND
BRINGER OF LIGHT

CONTENTS

CHAPTER 1

[TIM]
WAITING FOR MAKTEL

I am so scared. When Pleskit came to Earth, I never imagined I would end up being held in custody by an alien court on a planet hundreds of light-years from home.

Home. Boy, it seems so far away. Heck, it *is* so far away.

I wonder if I'll ever see it again.

Our law-speaker—the one helping Pleskit, Linnsy, Maktel, and me—says we should not be too worried. She says if we just write our statements, Judge Wingler will probably let us go. The Interplanetary Trading Federation just needs the information.

All the information.

The judge is letting us work together. And he wants us to start at the beginning, which means I should mention the *oog-slama*, and waiting for Maktel. He also wants us to be totally honest, even about our emotions, which is a little like being totally naked, if you ask me. But if that's what I have to do to get home — well, here goes . . .

"Mom!" I cried, running into the kitchen. "It moved! It moved!"

My mother turned off the blender and looked at me nervously. "What moved, Tim?"

"The *oog-slama*!"

An *oog-slama* is something like a cross between an egg and a cocoon, and it's one way shape-shifters on Hevi-Hevi reproduce. When Pleskit's Veeblax had created an *oog-slama*, Pleskit passed it on to me. If I could actually get the *oog-slama* to turn into a Veeblax, not only would I finally have a pet of my own, I'd be the only kid on Earth (besides Pleskit, of course) whose pet came from another planet!

What made this particularly nerve-racking was the fact that an *oog-slama* can take anywhere from five days to fifteen *years* to turn into a Veeblax! It's hard enough to wait for something when you know how long it's going to take. It's even worse when you have no idea when — or *if* — what you're waiting for will happen.

My mother followed me back to my room. We picked our way across the mess on the floor to my desk, where I was keeping the *oog-slama* in a padded bowl. Next to it was the spray bottle I was using to mist it several times a day.

The *oog-slama* looked like a three-inch-long purple pickle. Pleskit had told me that as a Veeblax-to-be matures, the skin of an *oog-slama* will sometimes become transparent. But as of right now the skin was still opaque, so I couldn't tell what (if anything) was happening inside it. That was one reason I had been so excited to see it move.

Mom and I stared at it for a long time.

Nothing happened.

"It *did* move," I said forlornly. "Honest. It twitched."

"That's all right, Tim," she said, putting her hand on my shoulder. "When I was pregnant with you, some-times I would feel you move. But when I tried to let your father feel it, you would stop, and might go a whole day before you did it again." She smiled. "You were stubborn even before you were born."

I shrugged. "Yeah, I suppose so."

She looked at me suspiciously. "All right, Timbo, what's going on? You've been acting pretty glum for the last couple of days."

"Nothing's wrong!" I said, a little too hastily.

She bent over so we were face-to-face. "Look me straight in the eyes and say that."

I couldn't do it, of course, and I was annoyed at her for trapping me like this. On the other hand, something inside me felt like it was going to explode, so maybe it would be just as well to let it out. Trying to sound casual, I shrugged and said, "I'm just a little worried about what will happen when Maktel gets here."

She looked surprised. "Why would you be worried about that? I thought when it came to aliens, your theory was 'the more the better.'"

Working to keep my voice from quavering, I said, "Mom, back on Hevi-Hevi, Maktel was Pleskit's best friend."

I hoped I wouldn't have to explain more, so I was

relieved when I saw the light go on in her eyes. "Ah," she said softly. "And now Pleskit is *your* best friend, and you don't know where you'll stand when his old best friend shows up for a visit."

I nodded, which was easier than trying to get any more words past the lump growing in my throat.

Mom took a deep breath. "Well, I can see why you would be wondering about that, honey. But I'm sure it will be fine."

"That's what mothers always say."

She made a face at me. "Have you talked to Pleskit about this?"

I looked at her as if she had lost her mind.

She pinched the top of her nose and sighed. "Tim, have you ever considered how weird it is for someone who thinks communication technology is the most interesting thing in the world to be so terrified by the idea of actually communicating?"

"You don't understand," I said.

"I never did," she replied, in a voice that let me know she was thinking of my father.

Words aren't the only way you can communicate.

She went back to her blender.

I sat down and stared at the *oog-slama*, trying not to think any more about Maktel's upcoming visit.

Actually, part of me really *was* excited about Maktel coming. After all, I had been wanting to meet him. But another part of me — a part that just wouldn't shut up — kept asking, *Am I truly Pleskit's best friend, or have I just been a temporary stand-in for the position?*

The question gnawed at my guts for the next two days. Friday afternoon, about an hour before Maktel was scheduled to arrive, I decided desperate measures were called for.

So I went upstairs to discuss the matter with Linnsy.

Linnsy *used* to be my best friend. But then she outgrew me, both socially and physically. We still get along okay, even if she does seem to think of me mostly as the doofus two floors down. Oddly enough, we've been getting along better since Pleskit arrived. I think it's because we've had to cooperate in order to survive a couple of times.

Anyway, Linnsy is very smart about social stuff, which is useful. Unfortunately, she doesn't have much patience for my *lack* of smartness in that regard, so getting advice from her usually means suffering through some nasty comments first — not to mention an occasional "punchie-wunchie," which is what she calls it when she socks me on the biceps to let me know I've said or done something particularly dorky.

I was prepared for all that.

What I wasn't prepared for was what I saw on her desk, which filled me with cold horror.

CHAPTER 2

[MAKTEL]
DEPARTURE FOR EARTH

Well I, for one, am glad that Judge Wingler has asked the four of us to write down everything that led to the mess the galactic media are now calling "The Earth-Based Catastrophe That Nearly Ended Life as We Know It." For one thing, it will prove that I was right to be suspicious.

Of course, it means I will also have to admit to some of the foolish things I did. But if that is what it takes to get out of here and back to Hevi-Hevi, I am willing to do so.

Actually, for me the story starts on Hevi-Hevi — or just above it, in a little shuttle craft.

Too Many Aliens

***

"Well, there it is, Maktel," said the Motherly One happily. "The ship that will carry you to Earth."

I stared through the window of our shuttle craft at the battered old freighter hanging in orbit above Hevi-Hevi. "But it's so . . . so *worn out*!" I said in dismay.

The Motherly One laughed, which I thought a rather cruel response. "The look of a ship will not necessarily tell you how well it works, Maktel. And the truth is, we didn't have many ships to choose from. After all, the Earth sector is hardly the kind of place major shippers find all that enticing—though if Meenom's mission is successful, that may change."

(For anyone not familiar with the details of the Earth mission, Meenom Ventrah is the Trader/Diplomat who currently holds the franchise on the planet. He is also Fatherly One to my friend Pleskit.)

I gazed at the freighter again. I was tremendously excited about the fact that I would be traveling to another planet on my own for the first time. I was also tremendously nervous. A somewhat less-well-worn vessel would have made me feel better about the trip, or at least my chances of surviving it.

"We were doubly lucky in finding this one," continued the Motherly One cheerfully, "as there is another passenger on board who is actually traveling right to Earth — a fact that reduces the fare considerably."

"Who is it?" I asked.

"The captain doesn't pass out that kind of information for free," said the Motherly One tartly. "However, as *yeeble* is traveling openly, I assume it is a friend or business partner of Pleskit's Fatherly One."

We had just docked at the side of the freighter. My feeling that the Motherly One was taking all this very lightly changed when we got inside. Suddenly she began to demonstrate uncharacteristic nervousness.

"Oh dear, Maktel," she said, looking around at the shabby corridors. "I hope this vessel is safe. I don't know if I can bear to let you go!"

I would have been startled, were I not so used to the Motherly One making sudden shifts of emotion for tactical advantage. I only wished I knew who the tactic was intended for. And tactical or not, I felt that the purple tears streaming out of her nose were inappropriate for a ranking member of the Hevi-Hevian Trading Council.

She knelt to embrace me. "It is hard for me to let you go, my little *bliddki*," she sobbed, her *sphen-gnut-ksher* drooping so severely that the knob almost touched her head.

I saw one of the crew members — a tall brown-and-orange being with four legs and more eyes than I could count — staring at us. I felt a surge of shame. I did not want to be the laughingstock of the entire crew for the duration of the trip — something I already feared because of my above-regulation level of pudginess.

"I will be fine, Motherly One," I said, trying to squirm free of her embrace and hoping desperately that she would not spend too much time weeping and wailing over my departure. Her carrying-on was stimulating my own fears, and I began to feel a surge of panic. So I was somewhat astonished when we entered my cabin and her demeanor suddenly changed again. Wiping the tears from her nose, she sat on the edge of my bunk, stared me straight in the face, and said calmly, "I have a task for you, Maktel."

"What is it, O Motherly One?" I asked, trying not to show my surprise. These sudden shifts were a way she had of preparing me for life as a diplomat.

"I need you to deliver a message to Pleskit's Fatherly One."

"Why don't you just send it by Galactanet?" I asked. "It would be faster."

She glanced around suspiciously, as if she feared we were being spied on. "Any message sent by electronic means can be captured and decoded. I want this to remain private."

My *sphen-gnut-ksher* emitted the spicy smell of shock. "Motherly One! I hope you are not contemplating a romance with Meenom Ventrah!"

It is hard to surprise the Motherly One. In this case I managed it. "Certainly not!" she cried. "This is strictly business. Honestly, Maktel, you are the most suspicious childling I have ever met."

"I've been well trained," I replied.

The Motherly One could not say much in response, as she knew this to be true. She is an extremely suspicious being. As if to change the subject, she reached into the pocket of her robe and pulled out a packet of *feebo beezbuds*.

"Yum!" I cried, reaching for it.

She snatched the packet away from my eager fingers. "You will ignore the sweetness inside here, Maktel," she said severely. "It is merely camouflage. The inside of this wrapper holds the message I want you to deliver to Meenom. I felt it was safer to wait until we were in your cabin to pass it on to you. Fewer spying eyes that way. I want you to pass it to Meenom the same way — in *complete* privacy. Is that clear?"

"Perfectly," I said, trying to hide my disappointment. The Motherly One does not like me to think about food too much.

She handed me the package, then leaned to embrace me, her *sphen-gnut-ksher* tapping mine in a Motherly One show of affection. "I shall miss you, my childling," she murmured gently. "I hope you will have a good trip. When you distribute our gifts to Meenom's staff, please also convey my best wishes to them."

Then she stood and strode from the room, leaving me as dazed, baffled, and amazed as I often am after a serious talk with the Motherly One. I thought about running after her, but did not want to give the crew anything further to tease me about. Besides, I knew her well enough to know that she was not going to give me any additional information. So I just sat there, trying to make sense of our conversation.

From the window of my little cabin I could see the shuttle leave the ship, carrying the Motherly One back toward the surface of Hevi-Hevi, which hung in its purple perfection against the black sky. I pressed my fingers to the window, wondering what I had been thinking of when I'd asked to be allowed to visit Earth on my own.

A short time later the *bloop-bloop* sounded, alerting everyone to prepare for leaving orbit. I lay on my bunk until the brief surge of acceleration was over. According to our schedule, we would reach the first *urpelli* in about half a ship's day. The trip through would be brief, of course, even though it would catapult us more than a hundred light-years from Hevi-Hevi. It would take eight ship's days, and six *urpelli* leaps, for us to reach Earth.

I thought about how good it would be to see Pleskit again. We share the bond common to all hatching mates, and I had mourned deeply when his Fatherly One had achieved diplomat status and begun the travels that took my friend from my side.

These thoughts slipped swiftly into nervousness about meeting his new friends, and concern about how I would fit in during my brief visit. My greatest worry, of course, had to do with Pleskit's friendship with the Earthboy Tim Tompkins. I had read with both excitement and jealousy the files Pleskit had sent me detailing their adventures. But now I wondered: *Am I still Pleskit's best friend, or is that now Tim's role? And how will I get along with this Earthling that Pleskit has grown so close to?*

All this thinking made me hungry, so I decided to go to the galley for a snack. Before I left my cabin, I opened one of my travel cases and carefully hid the Motherly One's secret message inside some underwear.

When I reached the galley, I found another passenger already sitting there — an elegant-looking being with blue skin and a beard of thick, writhing tentacles. He wore an ornate golden breastplate, a flowing crimson cape, and a ring that marked him as a full member of the Interplanetary Trading Federation. His headgear, which looked as if it were made of bronze, had a strange insignia on the front. A pair of extensions attached just behind the insignia angled backward, then made a sharp joint so that they thrust directly into his ears.

"Ah," he said when he saw me. "You must be the other passenger heading for Earth!"

Before I could respond, his headgear opened its eyes and said in a high, scratchy voice, "His name is Maktel, as you would know if you had been paying attention when we spoke to the captain."

CHAPTER 3

[MAKTEL]
ELLICO *VEC* BUR

The tall, elegant Trader laughed when he saw how startled I was by the fact that his headgear was alive. "Let us introduce ourselves," he said, rising to his feet. Making a sweeping bow, he said proudly, "We are Ellico *vec* Bur."

I tried not to look too surprised. I had heard of the *vecciri* before, of course. But this was the first time I had actually met one of these symbiotic duads.

The blue being extended his — their — hand for me to shake, saying, "I am the Ellico part of our selves." This meant, of course, that the bronze-shelled creature attached to his head must be Bur.

Too Many Aliens

Before I could say anything, Ellico put their right hand in front of my face, wiggled their fingers, then reached behind my ear and pulled out a *snergal*. As they handed me the shiny coin, Bur said, "We're glad to find we're not the only ones going to this sad backwater of a planet. It will be good to have company."

"What is taking you to Earth?" I asked.

"Business," said the Ellico portion, returning to their seat.

Before they could say more, we were interrupted by a green waiter-bot rolling in with the Trader(s)'

order. It was served on a plate mounted on long legs that raised it to just beneath their chin. I understood the reason for the legs when one of Ellico *vec* Bur's beard-tentacles reached out and grabbed a pod off the plate. Two other tentacles pried the pod open. A fourth pulled out the slimy nugget inside and popped it into Ellico's mouth. While he was chewing, Bur took up the conversation.

"The ambassador and we went to school together. We have not seen him in many *grinnugs*, but he contacted us recently in regard to an exciting business possibility—exporting something called 'peanut butter,' which he thinks is going to cause quite a stir in the galaxy. We are looking forward to discussing it with him."

"I know about peanut butter," I said. "My friend Pleskit was the one who discovered its strange properties."

I did not mention that this discovery—that peanut butter made Hevi-Hevians wildly, passionately romantic—had nearly gotten Pleskit thrown out of school. It was possible that Ellico *vec* Bur did not know this, and one does not give out all one's information too cheaply.

"Ah, Pleskit," said the Ellico portion, which had finished chewing the pod. "We fear our arrival will be somewhat disturbing to him. He is not entirely fond of us."

I started to ask why Pleskit didn't like Ellico *vec* Bur, but the Trader(s) raised a hand to cut off the question. "It is not our story to tell," said the Ellico part.

I hate that kind of comment. However, it was about the only annoying thing Ellico *vec* Bur did during the entire journey. The duad had the charm that is part of virtually every Trader's personal tool kit, and for most of the trip they entertained me with fanciful stories from their home planets and various bits of hand magic. Their cloak seemed to hold innumerable devices for performing tricks and jokes, some of them slightly naughty. The one they called "The Farting Ambassador" was my favorite, and never failed to send me into gales of laughter.

I welcomed these diversions, especially as our ship drew closer to Earth and my fears began to take deeper root in my mind.

I was still terribly excited about seeing Pleskit, of course. But the stories he had sent me of life on this primitive and semi-barbaric planet had me wondering what strange and terrifying things might happen during my visit.

The closer we came to the time of our arrival, the more distressed I became. I checked my pack over and over to make sure the guesting gifts I had for the embassy staff were all ready. And several times a day I examined the mysterious package of *feebo beezbuds* the Motherly One had asked me to carry to Meenom. What could the message be?

Curiosity consumed me and I was dying to open the package. I was also dying to consume what was inside it. But I knew that opening it would be improper. Besides, if I did succumb to my curiosity, the Motherly One would be sure to find out. She is inescapable in that way.

I ate most of my meals with Ellico *vec* Bur, and though the Trader(s)' behavior was unfailingly polite, they asked more questions than I wanted to answer. They seemed especially interested in the Motherly One and anything she might have said to me before she left the ship. They were cagey with these questions, and expressed them mostly by talking about her distress, and their desire that she not be too worried about me. Even so, they caused me to be suspicious.

Finally the day came when the ship entered Earth orbit.

"Well, this is it, Maktel," said Ellico *vec* Bur jovially as we brought out our luggage and took our place in the transport pod that would carry us down to the surface.

The pod was piloted by the four-legged crew member I had noticed when the Motherly One had first led me aboard the freighter.

The planet we saw waiting below us was surprisingly beautiful, a mottled blue ball with an unusual amount of surface water. I wondered if the Earthlings had any idea how lucky they were to possess such an abundance of this resource.

Soon we saw the embassy dangling from its support hook atop a hill made white by a dusting of snow. The embassy's familiar design — Pleskit says the Earthlings claim it looks like a "flying saucer" — instantly made me feel more at home.

The pod swept under the embassy to dock at the little port located on its lower side. I heard the magnetic click that indicated the seal was complete.

"Ready?" asked Ellico *vec* Bur as the top of the pod opened.

Without waiting for my answer, the Trader(s) stood on the mag-pad that would lift them into the embassy. As they started to rise out of the pod, the crew member who had piloted us down put a hand on my arm. He waited until the Trader(s) were gone, then leaned to me and whispered, "I'd watch out for them if I were you."

"What do you mean?" I asked.

But he just crossed his eyes in a gesture for silence and discretion, and pointed to the mag-pad.

I climbed on, and floated up into the embassy.

CHAPTER 4

[LINNSY]
HOW TO HURT A FRIEND

So now it's my turn. All right, I guess the real starting point for me was the afternoon of Maktel's arrival. I was sitting at my desk having a very pleasant daydream when my mother shouted, "Linnsy! Mr. Timothy is here to see you!"

I have no idea why my mother calls Tim "Mr. Timothy." It's just one of her little quirks.

She's got a lot of them.

When I didn't answer right away, she shouted, "Linnsy!"

I sighed. "All right, Mom. I'm coming."

I pushed myself away from my desk without looking

at what I had been doodling while I daydreamed. Too bad; I might have saved a lot of trouble if I had bothered to glance down.

Tim was sitting on the living room couch. He looked so upset, I wondered if someone had finally told him that the people on *Tarbox Moon Warriors* were only actors.

"What happened to you?" I asked.

"I need to talk."

"About what?"

"It's private."

I sighed yet again, then said, "All right, let's go to my room."

This was my second mistake. I should probably just ban Tim from my room altogether. I'd have a good excuse, since his mother is starting to get antsy about the two of us having private conferences in either of our rooms. My own mother is more calm about this, mostly because she knows that my romantic interest in Tim is about equal to my desire to pound large nails into my head. But I tend to give in easily when he has that wounded-puppy look on his face, partly because I still have some guilt about the way I sort of stopped talking to him for a while back in fifth grade because he was such a doofus. But we've lived in the same apartment building forever and we used to sort of be best friends, so I started feeling pretty rotten about that. And after the aliens came to live in Syracuse, we faced several problems we had to work together to solve.

So now we're friends again, sort of. And the poor guy was obviously so upset that refusing to listen to him would have been like refusing to put a goldfish that's flopped out of its tank back into the water.

When we got to my room, I sat down at my desk, feeling a little like Lucy, the five-cent psychiatrist in the *Peanuts* comic strip.

Tim plunked himself down in my beanbag chair.

"Well?" I said.

His eyes darted around the room, looking anywhere but at me. He'd gone from wounded puppy to trapped animal. I had been through this with him before, so I just sat and waited. Finally he blurted, "I'm worried about what's going to happen when Maktel gets here."

Tim's a boy, so you have to translate when he's talking about emotional stuff, and it took me a minute to work this one out. As I was thinking about it, I glanced down at my desk.

A cold surge of horror twisted my stomach when I saw my daydream doodles.

I started to blush and moved my hand to cover the paper. But my hand wasn't big enough, and the gesture was too suspicious. Tim raised himself in the chair to look at my desk. When he saw what I was trying to hide, his eyes widened and he turned as red as I suspect I was already. He looked sick.

"Sorry," he muttered bitterly. "I didn't mean to bother you."

Then he leaped up and bolted out of my room.

"Tim!" I cried. *"Wait!"*

He didn't, of course, and a second later I heard the door to the hall open and slam shut.

I collapsed in my chair and stared with disgust at the paper under my fingers.

Scrawled across it in a dozen different kinds of fancy writing was "Jordan Lynch Jordan Lynch Jordan Lynch."

I wanted to scream. What the heck was going on here? I have better things to do with my time than obsess about a guy who's the biggest snot in our class.

On the other hand, even though Jordan seems to be taking a correspondence class in butt-headedness, he's also the only boy in our school who's as tall as I am. And at my height — I'm the official class Amazon — that has to count for something.

And, to be honest, he's a genuine hottie.

I was working on a theory that a lot of the reason why Jordan acts so nasty is that his parents pretty much ignore him, except to buy him stuff. My theory is that he's just trying to mask the deep pain tearing at his heart.

Whatever the reason, I couldn't seem to get him out of my mind, and it was driving me nuts. It was as if I had a little war going on inside me. Part of me wanted to stop thinking about Jordan altogether. But another part kept saying, *Maybe all he needs is the right girl to get him on track.* With my help, Jordan could probably be class president when we get to high school. I imagined us going to the prom together, being voted class couple, driving off to —

I shook my head in disgust. Why couldn't I get these stupid ideas out of my head? My mother had thought she could fix my father, and look how that turned out!

None of this, of course, was anything that I could ever discuss with Tim. When Jordan got put in our class after he got kicked out of the fancy private school where he used to go, for some reason he chose Tim to be his personal psychic punching bag. Tim has suffered a lot from Jordan since then — which meant that just having these thoughts made me feel incredibly disloyal.

But that upset me too. I mean, what was Tim to me that I should worry about what he thought?

I started to wad up the paper, then smoothed it out and slid it into my desk.

As I did, a new question occurred to me, a truly horrifying one: What if Tim told someone — *anyone* — what he had seen?

I moaned, and wondered if I could talk my parents into moving.

CHAPTER 5

[PLESKIT]
ANXIETY

The silvery walls of this place are beautiful but cold. I wish nothing more than to go home. Even my new home on Earth would be better than this.

The key to release is simple, yet painful. I must tell, clearly and honestly, my part of the story. At least, I hope that will be sufficient to set us free.

I am glad that Judge Wingler is allowing us to work together. Even so, it is not easy to write down not only the facts of what happened but also the secret workings of the *smorgle*.

Across the room, in a beam of light, I can see Maktel, working on his part of the story. Perhaps writing this down will help me understand how I came into conflict with someone whom I care for so much.

Tim showed me what he has written so far. It made me sad to read it. And Linnsy — well, I am not ready to talk about what happened to Linnsy.

Like the others, I guess I should choose a starting point. Perhaps it was when I returned to the embassy after school on the day Maktel was to arrive.

McNally and I went to the kitchen as usual.

Barvgis, the round and slimy being who acts as assistant to the Fatherly One, was there already. This was not surprising. The kitchen is his favorite place.

The room smelled wonderful because Shhh-foop, our Queen of the Kitchen, had prepared a fresh batch of *finnikle-pokta*. "Just for you, my little Pleskit-pingle," she sang, sliding to the table and placing them in front of me.

The oozy things squeaked and rolled about the platter in a most appetizing way. Even so, I had no desire to eat anything right then.

Before I could think of how to tell this to Shhh-foop, she slid back to the counter. She returned an instant later, this time clutching a steaming pot of black liquid in two of her orange tentacles. In a third she held an empty cup. The rest of her tentacles vibrating with eagerness, she warbled, "Some coffee for the handsome Just McNally?"

She calls him that because McNally does not like to use his first name. When he is introduced to someone, he always says, "The name's McNally — just McNally." This led Shhh-foop to think his name was "Just McNally," an idea she has never been able to shake.

My Earthling bodyguard glanced up at her. His eyes were hidden by his ever-present sunglasses. Even so, I could sense his panic. McNally loves coffee, but for some reason our Queen of the Kitchen has never been able to master the secrets of this Earthly beverage.

"I have devised a new method for wringing joyous flavor from the bean of caffeine in order to bring happiness to your tongue," she sang. Her notes were hopeful, yet colored by a tragic undertone of longing mixed with anxiety.

"Sure," said McNally gruffly. "I'll try a cup, Shhh-foop."

"Oh, *glorptious* glee!" she trilled, pouring fragrant liquid into the cup. She placed it in front of him.

McNally took a sniff and smiled hopefully. "Smells

good!" He blew across the top of the cup, then raised it to his lips.

Shhh-foop wrapped her tentacles around herself, quivering with excitement. McNally took a sip. Shhh-foop watched with wide eyes, waiting for his approval.

Alas, it was not to be. Suddenly McNally flinched. He began to twitch, then shook his head violently, as if trying to dislodge a *tigloop* from his ear. *"Whooo-eee!"* he cried. Taking a deep breath, he carefully set the cup on the table, then slid it as far away as his arm would reach.

Shhh-foop was wringing her tentacles in agony.

"Not . . . ," gasped McNally, his voice a husky whisper, "quite."

Tentacles drooping, Shhh-foop slid back to the counter, singing "The Lament of the Coffee Bean," a song of despair that has grown to several hundred verses since she first began composing it.

"It was kind of you to try a taste," I said, putting my hand on my bodyguard's arm.

"Sure," he said — well, whispered; his voice still did not seem to be working properly. Then he glanced down at my plate of *finnikle-pokta*. Without speaking, he pointed at it, then lifted an eyebrow.

Too Many Aliens

I have learned that this is an Earthling way of asking a question. And I knew very well what he was asking: Why was my food, which happened to be something I like very much, untouched?

I shrugged, an Earthling gesture I had picked up from prolonged exposure to the species. "I don't feel like eating."

"Why not?" asked Barvgis. The idea of someone not wanting to eat always puzzles Barvgis, mostly because it is a feeling he has never personally experienced.

"Anxiety and nervousness are tying a knot in my *kirgiltum*."

"Someone been bugging you at school?" asked McNally protectively. His voice seemed to be recovering from Shhh-foop's latest creation.

I waggled my *sphen-gnut-ksher* to indicate that this idea was wrong.

Barvgis looked at me slyly. "Does this have anything to do with Maktel's impending arrival?" He scooped a large handful of squirmers out of the bowl in front of him. Ignoring their tiny screams, he poured them into his gaping mouth.

Unlike the squirmers, I made no sound at all. However, my silence answered Barvgis's question quite clearly.

"What are you so nervous about?" asked McNally in surprise. "I thought Maktel was your best bud."

"He is. At least, he was my best bud on Hevi-Hevi. But I also have a best bud here on Earth."

"Ah," said McNally. "I've got the picture. You're worried about having two best buds in the same place. I understand. Happened to me with a couple of lady friends once." He shook his head. "I gotta tell you, it wasn't pretty."

"I think I am too young to hear about your romances, McNally," I said.

Though I had not intended the statement to be funny, it caused Barvgis to laugh so hard, he nearly choked on a squirmer.

I went to my room to play with the Veeblax. But even the antics of my little shape-shifter could not distract me. By the time Maktel's ship was due, I was so excited I thought my head was going to explode.

(I must point out to Judge Wingler that I learned this bizarrely violent phrase from Tim. The fact that I feel comfortable using it—in fact, didn't even notice I *had* used it until I looked back on what I have already written—may indicate I already have spent too much time on my new planet.)

Too Many Aliens

Time passed so slowly that I began to think someone had murdered the clock. (Gak! There's another one!) I was sitting in my room, wondering if I should make a visit to *Wakkam* Akkim, the Fatherly One's spiritual massagemaster, when the speaker above my door belched for attention.

"Transport pod approaching! Anticipated docking time: two minutes and forty-seven seconds."

Maktel was here at last!

Shoving aside my concerns, I hurried to greet my friend. Though I was first to arrive, the rest of the staff soon entered as well—everyone from Ms. Buttsman, the prim and proper Earthling who acts as our protocol adviser, to Beezle Whompis, the Fatherly One's personal secretary, an energy being who only takes physical form as an occasional act of courtesy to those around him.

The Fatherly One was there, of course. To my surprise, he had even brought the brain of the Grandfatherly One.

"Pod connected!" announced the speaker.

I was hugging myself with anticipation. But when the tube from the dock opened, I stepped back in dismay.

CHAPTER 6

[PLESKIT]
GIFTS AND GREETINGS

"I did not know you were coming," I said when I saw Ellico *vec* Bur step out of the tube that carries guests up from the docking pad.

The Trader(s) bowed their mutual head. "Perhaps your Fatherly One was too busy to mention it, Pleskit," said the Ellico portion. "It's nice to see you again too."

My *sphen-gnut-ksher* twitched in embarrassment as I returned their bow. "I am sorry. That was not a very polite greeting. It is good to see you, Ellico *vec* Bur."

This was a lie, but such little lies are an important part of the diplomatic life.

The Trader(s) nodded and moved aside. To my dis-

38

tress, the tube was now empty. Before I could get too worried, the mag-pad floated up. On it stood Maktel. He was dressed in a traditional Hevi-Hevian travel robe, and though most of his luggage would be carried up by the scurry-bots, he had a pack on his back.

At the sight of him I cried out in joy and ran forward.

He leaped out of the tube to greet me. We embraced, then did an interpretive dance to express our delight at seeing each other.

It was a relief to be able to dance this way again.

I had not done so for some time, mostly because I learned shortly after my arrival on Earth that my class-mates were baffled and amused by such behavior. It is not pleasant to be expressing your deepest feelings and have people roar with laughter as a result.

The Veeblax joined our dance, capering around in a shape a little like an Earthling cat, except for the wings.

When we finished the dance, my friend tapped his *sphen-gnut-ksher* against mine and said, "I have brought a guesting gift for you. In fact," he contin-ued, taking his pack from his back and opening it, "I have gifts for everyone." The staff applauded, as was appropriate. Even McNally and Ms. Buttsman joined in, though they looked somewhat puzzled.

Maktel rummaged in his pack for a moment, then pulled out a package wrapped in golden paper. "This is for you," he said happily.

I tore it open and cried out in excitement. He had brought the most recent issues of three of our favor-ite Terror-ramas: *Scum-suckers from Frizbat Twelve, The Fertile Energybeast*, and *True Stories of Diplomatic Errors*.

"Thank you, O Friendly One!" I cried. "I can't wait to

pop these onto my *sphen-gnut-ksher* and savor the fear."

"You'd better share," he said jovially. Then he reached into his pack for another gift. Watching him, I thought of the Earth character Santa Claus, who is also pudgy and carries a pack of gifts.

"Shhh-foop, this is from both me and the Motherly One," he said, handing our Queen of the Kitchen a set of glossy purple containers.

"Fresh spices!" she sang, twirling her tentacles with joy. "Oh, I shall make loveliness for the tongue with these!"

For Barvgis he had brought a vibrating belly band.

"I've wanted one of these since my last one broke!" cried Barvgis. He strapped the purple band around his waist, then chortled with delight as it caused his roundness to jiggle.

Maktel turned to my bodyguard. "You must be McNally," he said.

"Guilty as charged," replied McNally.

Maktel looked puzzled.

"It's an Earthling expression," I whispered.

"Ah," he said. "I am only partway through the learning program." He turned back to McNally. "Pleskit has told me much about you. The Motherly One and I thought carefully about what I should bring you." He reached into his pack and drew forth a pair of sunglasses. "I hope you will like these. You can use them night and day, since they will let you see very clearly even in complete darkness."

After passing the glasses to McNally, Maktel leaned to me and said quietly, "The Motherly One and I checked the technology; it is low level enough that it is permissible to give them to an Earthling."

I nodded in relief. I had sent an image of Earthling sunglasses to Maktel for his Motherly One to feed to the design machine. I was glad our little surprise had worked out.

"Very cool!" said McNally, slipping them on.

"They'll warm up," said Maktel. Then he made the small burp of embarrassment and said, "Oh, yes—that other kind of cool that Pleskit has told me about."

"Yeah, that kind," said McNally. "These definitely qualify. Can't wait till it's dark so I can try them out!"

"And now for the estimable Ms. Buttsman. The Motherly One and I thought you might like this." From his pack he pulled a printed copy of *The Complete Guide to Interplanetary Protocol*, Second Revised Edition.

"Why, Maktel!" said Ms. Buttsman, with more enthusiasm than I had ever before heard from her. "What a lovely and *appropriate* gift. Thank you!"

My friend continued to distribute goodies from his pack. Beezle Whompis received some energy snacks — a welcome gift for someone who has no actual physical presence. They were blue spheres that fizzed and crackled in their bag. "Wonderful!" cried Beezle Whompis. He tossed one into his mouth, and a glow of blue energy surrounded him.

"For you, *Wakkam* Akkim, I have brought this," said Maktel, taking a small pouch made of soft green material from his pack. I could tell from the look of it that it was filled with money. This was good, as that is what holy beings like best.

The short, feathery woman fluttered her eyebrows to show her appreciation and respect.

"I have something for you, too, Ambassador Meenom," Maktel said, reaching yet again into his pack.

But the Fatherly One was gone, as was Ellico *vec* Bur.

The look on Maktel's face when he realized this startled and frightened me.

CHAPTER 7

[MAKTEL]
URPELLI AND INSULTS

I was very disturbed when Ellico *vec* Bur spirited Ambassador Meenom away before I could present him with my guesting gift. Did the Trader(s) know I was carrying a secret message? Were they trying to prevent me from delivering it?

The odd thing was, at that moment I was only going to give Meenom a small jar of water from the Sea of Illakamin. After all, the Motherly One had specifically told me to pass on her message only in total privacy. Even so, the way Ellico *vec* Bur had managed to keep me from giving *anything* to the ambassador made me suspicious.

44

Too Many Aliens

The moment of awkward silence when I realized the ambassador was gone was broken by Shhh-foop, clapping her tentacles together and warbling, "Snacks! I have snacks for the weary traveler."

And not just any snacks. Shhh-foop is famous throughout the Hevi-Hevian diplomatic community for her *finnikle-pokta.* My *kirgiltum* began to twitch at the very thought of them.

After we had eaten, Pleskit showed me to my room. The scurry-bots had already delivered my luggage.

"You looked disturbed at not being able to present your gift to the Fatherly One," Pleskit said as he helped me unpack.

"I do not entirely trust Ellico *vec* Bur," I replied. "I suspect they were trying to keep me from passing anything to your parental unit."

Pleskit made the stinky smell of cynicism. "I have no love for those Trader(s). Even so, I think you are being too suspicious, Maktel."

"And just why don't you like them?" I asked.

"A bad experience quite some time ago," he replied evasively. "But that is old history."

"Old history or not, it seems to me that suspicion

45

is justified. You yourself said that your Fatherly One is concerned about an unexpected and unexplained amount of traffic in the Earth area."

"I don't see what that would have to do with Ellico *vec* Bur," said Pleskit. "Let's talk about what we're going to do while you're here. The first thing is, I've invited Tim to come over tomorrow."

"Good! I will be glad to finally meet him."

Though I said this enthusiastically, I was filled with trepidation. So I was ready, probably, to view Tim with a critical eye.

I suppose it is possible that was part of the reason our meeting the next day went so badly. However, I think the bulk of the blame must go to Tim.

It was late morning when he arrived, and Shhh-foop kindly offered us some snacks.

To my disgust, Tim was undiplomatically fussy about this.

"I haven't had terribly good luck with alien food," he explained.

"Ah, yes," I replied. "I remember reading how you . . . what is the Earthling word? Oh yes! *Puked*. I remember reading how you puked *finnikle-pokta* all over the evil

Mikta-makta-mookta. I thought that was very funny."

"It wasn't funny at the time," said Tim grimly. "I'd been wondering what you thought of the stories of our adventures that Pleskit has been sending you. We've been through a lot together, eh, Pleskit?"

I felt a twist in my *gnorzle*.

"You were asking me the other day about how I sent those stories," said Pleskit quickly. "Maybe Maktel should tell you. He's very good at that kind of thing."

He was obviously changing the subject, though whether it was to keep from embarrassing Tim, himself, or me, I could not tell. But it was a good change. I know a lot about interstellar communication, and I was happy to share my knowledge.

"The system works a little like what you Earthlings call the Internet," I said. "We have hundreds of thousands of stations that forward communications according to a master routing program. But standard transmissions can only flow at the speed of light, of course. That's fast enough for local things — ships that are only a few million miles apart, even planets that are part of the same solar system. But it would be impossibly slow for interstellar distances. Can you imagine? Sending a message from Earth to the nearest star and getting a reply would take more than eight of your years. And to send a message from one side of the galaxy to the other and get a reply would take hundreds of thousands!"

"So what do you do instead?" asked Tim.

"Our ships make time/space jumps through twists in space that we call *urpelli*."

"Is that something like a wormhole?" asked Tim.

I glanced at Pleskit. He closed his eyes, and I could see he was searching his brain for a reference. "Close enough," he said after a moment. "Not quite the same, but the idea works."

"Well, anyway," I continued, "we also send messages through the *urpelli*. But even that would leave many areas of the galaxy long separated and deeply isolated, if it were not for the Grand *Urpelli*."

"What's that?" asked Tim eagerly.

I smiled, warming to my subject. "For some reason — no one knows why, exactly — many *urpelli* are linked to a single giant *urpelli*."

"Well, it's not really a giant," interrupted Pleskit. "No one can figure out the exact size of an *urpelli* anyway."

"That is true," I said, feeling a little cranky and

wishing I had finished the language program before arriving. "The point is, most *urpelli* have two 'ends' at two different points in the galaxy. The weird thing is, almost all of them also connect to the Grand *Urpelli.*"

"So how do you know which place you're going to come out?" asked Tim.

"It took a long time to figure that out. But we now have ships and message devices that can handle that. As a result, because so many of the *urpelli* link to the Grand *Urpelli,* the vastness of the galaxy is tamed. In fact, the longest communication time in the galaxy is no more than about fourteen of your Earthling days. It makes any other way of trying to communicate seem quite primitive."

"Yeah, I guess so," said Tim.

He suddenly sounded a little sullen. I figured this was due to him being jealous because his planet is so far behind us.

"Do not be downhearted," I said consolingly. "Your people will come along eventually."

"So we can be just like you?" snarled Tim. (Pleskit insists it was not a snarl, but it certainly sounded that way to me.)

"Don't worry," I said coolly, not responding to his vicious tone. "You have a long way to go before that will happen."

Pleskit cracked his knuckles in disapproval, a signal that Tim would not understand.

His gesture startled me, and I realized, with some surprise, how insulting I had been. I cursed myself, hardly able to believe I had said something so undip-lomatic. The Motherly One would not have been proud. Unfortunately, the damage had been done, and I was caught in a relationship web I could not break at the moment.

Tim left not long afterward.

Our parting was cold and unpleasant.

After he was gone, Pleskit looked at me angrily. "What was that all about?"

"What do you mean?"

"You were needlessly insulting," he said, farting the small but pungent fart of disapproval.

"Who cares what such a primitive being thinks any-way?" I snapped.

Then I fled to my room, feeling stupid, ashamed, and very, very far from home.

CHAPTER 8

[TIM]
REGRETS AND CONFUSIONS

I walked away from Pleskit's room wondering how he could possibly have a creep like Maktel for a friend. To be honest, I was having a hard time not crying.

Then I saw something that startled me — an alien I had never met before. I knew everyone on the staff. Was it possible the embassy had another visitor that Pleskit had not mentioned? Or — and this thought chilled me — was this some spy or invader?

The alien was blue, with a face that was fairly human except for his beard, which was made of finger-thick tentacles that seemed to move on their own. He wore an elegant jacket and a golden breastplate, and carried an ornate walking stick. Mounted on his head was a bronze cap with two weird things that stuck out from the front, angling toward the back of his head. They looked like long crab legs. A "knee" toward the back of them bent them so that they stuck directly into his ears.

The blue guy smiled when he saw me, and motioned for me to come closer.

I wasn't sure what to do. Much as I have always been fascinated by outer space stuff, after my visit with Maktel, I had had enough of aliens for one day.

"You are Tim, are you not?" asked the alien.

I nodded.

"Then we are very pleased to meet you. We are Ellico *vec* Bur."

"We?" I asked, curious in spite of myself.

I almost squawked when his bronze cap opened its eyes and said in a high, scratchy voice, "Well, there *are* two of us here, even if we are in a permanent state of union."

The blue being smiled. "We take it you've never met one of the *vecciri*—the, ah . . . *joined* ones. Bur and I are life partners. I provide locomotion."

"And I provide enhanced intelligence," said Bur.

Ellico looked a little annoyed. "Anyway, we did not stop you to discuss biology."

"Why did you stop me? And how did you know my name?"

Bur made a little noise that I took to be disgust at my stupidity, though maybe I was just feeling sensitive at the moment. Ellico said, "The ambassador mentioned we might see an Earthling youngster wandering around the embassy. He also told us a little about you. He spoke very highly of the support and help you have given Pleskit."

I began to feel a little better.

Ellico *vec* Bur glanced around, then leaned toward me a little. Lowering their voices, they said simultaneously, "We are here to discuss some business with the ambassador. We won't be around very long. Even so, we're a little concerned about how things might be going for Meenom. Keep your eyes open for anything suspicious happening around the city, would you?"

"Like what?" I asked, intrigued now.

The Ellico part raised an eyebrow and said, "We think there may be other off-worlders here, up to no good."

"Shouldn't I just tell Meenom if I think I spot anything like that?"

"Of course," said the Trader(s) quickly and simultaneously. "We're not suggesting you keep anything from the ambassador. We just wanted to ask you to stay, as you Earthlings put it, 'on your toes.' Very pleased to meet you, Earthling Tim."

And with that they tapped me gently on the head with their cane and strolled past.

They were whistling, though since I was behind them now, I couldn't tell which of them was making the sound.

Maybe it was both.

Ralph-the-Driver took me home in the embassy limo. He didn't say anything along the way. He never does.

As we drove, I tried to think about the conversation with Ellico *vec* Bur, which seemed important. But to be honest it was the way things had worked out with Maktel that was really on my mind. Clearly he was a snot and a snob, and the two of us weren't going to get along.

I tried to slip into the apartment without Mom noticing.

No such luck.

Too Many Aliens

"How'd it go, hon?" she called from her bedroom.

I went to her door. She was sitting at her sewing machine.

"Okay," I said.

She knew immediately that the whole thing had rotted, of course. She's like that.

"So, what went wrong?" she asked.

I shrugged. "Maktel's a booger."

She actually laughed, which I didn't appreciate. "Don't take it too hard, Tim. Three can be a tricky number when it comes to friendship. It just seems to be human nature."

"Nice try, Mom, but Pleskit and Maktel aren't human."

My mother sighed. "You know what I mean."

I did, but I didn't want to talk about it. Besides, when she starts with "you know what I mean," there's not much point in talking anyway, since she's got her mind made up. Fortunately, she changed the subject on her own. "Look," she said proudly.

She held up a little bag made of white mesh. It had a drawstring at the top, and two black straps.

"You made it!" I cried.

She smiled. "It seemed like a good idea."

The purpose of the bag was to let me keep the *oog-slama* close to me. According to the little booklet Pleskit had printed out from volume 4,658 of the *Encyclopedia Galactica*, carrying the Veeblax-to-be around would help it bond to me.

"Come on," said Mom. "Let's see if the bag is the right size. Then I'll help you strap it on."

We went to my room and tucked the *oog-slama* into the little bag. It fit perfectly. Mom showed me how to put on the straps — one over my shoulder, one around my chest, so that the *oog-slama* was nestled slightly above my armpit.

"It's just right!" I said happily. "Thank you!"

She gave me a little hug. "Glad you like it."

She had only been out of the room for a few minutes when the *oog-slama* wiggled. I was really happy when that happened. But it also made me a little sad, because I didn't feel I could call Pleskit to tell him about it.

Why didn't he do something to help? I asked myself, which was when I realized that I was almost as mad at him as I was at Maktel.

I tried to stuff that feeling down. Pleskit and I

had already had one bust-up, and I didn't want to go through it again. Besides, if I got mad at him now, he had Maktel to hang out with, so maybe he would just forget me as a friend altogether.

Of course, Maktel wasn't here permanently; his visit was only supposed to last three weeks. Once he left, Pleskit would be on his own again. Let him come crawling back looking for a friend then! Ha!

Except I knew I would still be glad to be his friend. Which confused me, since it almost made me wonder if what he had said once when he was upset—that I was just being his friend because I'm so crazy about the idea of aliens — was true.

But I knew it wasn't; I liked Pleskit just for who he was.

Which meant I should probably do the best I could to get along with the brat Maktel while he was here.

I wished I could go talk to Linnsy about this. But I was still upset with her, on account of the business with Jordan. (Not to mention the fact that she was also annoyed with me, and might not be willing to talk to me anyway.}

I was relieved when Pleskit called on the comm-device to make peace. Only, when he tried to tell me that the situation with Maktel was partly my fault, I got angry and hung up.

The call upset me so much that I decided to swallow my pride and go talk to Linnsy — even if it did mean a few punchie-wunchies. (And that's not even counting the fact that I would have to apologize for the way I'd acted the last time I'd gone to see her, even though the thought of her and Jordan together made my stomach feel like it had the day when I'd eaten the *finnikle-pokta*.)

CHAPTER 9

[PLESKIT]
DISTRESS AND MYSTERY

After my call to Tim went so badly, I was more distressed than ever. I decided it was time to seek advice on the matter.

The first person I wanted to speak to was the Fatherly One, as that is the appropriate thing to do in such matters. Unfortunately, he was tied up in a conference with the president of Botswana.

"I'm not sure when he'll be through," said Beezle Whompis, who had flickered into sight just to talk to me. "He said it was going to be a difficult conversation."

He reached into his desk and took out one of the energy snacks Maktel had given him. "These are quite a treat," he said, popping it into his mouth. Immediately he was surrounded by an aura of blue light. "Ah!" he said, once the crackling sound had died down. "That was *good*!"

"I will tell Maktel you like his gift," I said.

What I did not say was how much it pained me that the Fatherly One was once again unavailable. *Wakkam* Akkim had guided my parental unit and myself through many conversations on this topic. I understood his responsibilities. But understanding did not make the emptiness I felt any less painful.

I decided to try the Grandfatherly One next. Ever since his death, we have kept his brain in a clear vat filled with an electrolyte solution that keeps him comfortable. As a sign of respect, he has his own room, which is where I went.

To my surprise, I found not only the Grandfatherly One there but *Wakkam* Akkim as well. The small, bird-like woman had taken off her cloak, which was fluttering nearby. She was sitting cross-legged in front of the brainvat, chanting in a high-pitched voice.

"I'm sorry," I said. "I did not mean to interrupt."

"No problem," said the Grandfatherly One through the black speakers mounted on either side of the brainvat. "What do you want, youngling?"

I bowed my head. "I have a problem I wish to discuss, O Venerated One."

Wakkam Akkim stood. "I will leave, if you wish."

"Stay, stay," said the Grandfatherly One. "The sprout could do worse than get advice from one of the wisest beings in the galaxy."

"Unwarranted flattery is like a raindrop falling into the ocean," said the *wakkam*. "Quickly absorbed, quickly forgotten."

"Yeah, yeah, yeah. Cut me some slack, will ya? I'm dead, for Pete's sake. Let's just see what Pleskit wants."

"Some advice," I said.

"Well, I'm glad *someone* wants my advice," snorted the Grandfatherly One. "Your Fatherly One might as well have let me go to my final rest for all the times he actually consults me."

"And how much time spent you with he, when he was but a sprout?" asked the *wakkam* softly.

"If you weren't such a wise and holy being, I'd throw you out of here," said the Grandfatherly One, sounding distinctly uncomfortable. "Why don't you save some of that advice for Pleskit?"

"What is your problem?" asked the *wakkam*, turning to me.

"Tim and Maktel do not seem to like each other. Their first meeting went very badly."

"Oy," said the Grandfatherly One, employing one of his favorite Earthly expressions. "You probably should have skipped me and gone straight to *Wakkam* Akkim anyway. This kind of thing is her specialty."

"I felt I should seek the wisdom of my family first," I replied.

"When it comes to this kind of thing, your family is not all that wise," said the Grandfatherly One. "Take your parental unit. Please. He may be a genius at diplomacy, but he's a total *fushloob* at applying what he knows to personal situations."

I made the smell of confusion. "That seems silly."

"It *is* silly," replied the Grandfatherly One. "Many true things are silly."

I turned to *Wakkam* Akkim. "Can you help me in this perplexity?"

She put her hands together and bowed her head. "Do you feel it is your job to solve it?" she asked.

I paused to think about this. "No, not my job," I said

at last. "But I would be happier if it were solved."

"Why?"

This seemed pretty obvious, but the *wakkamami* work in mysterious ways. "If my friends fight, we will not have fun together. I would like Maktel's visit to be fun."

"Fun is good," agreed the *wakkam*. "What were they fighting about?"

"That is hard to say. It didn't seem to be about anything real to me. Maktel, who is usually polite, said some insulting things. Tim, who is usually easygoing, got quite angry about them."

The feathers of the *wakkam*'s eyebrows waved gracefully. "If the fight was not about what it seemed to be about, it is likely it was about something else."

"But what?" I cried, beginning to grow frustrated.

"Conflicts often arise when two beings want something and each fears the other will be the one to get it."

"What kind of something?"

"What do both boys want?" asked the *wakkam*. "Answer that, and you've got a good start."

She trilled a whistle, and the little winged things

attached to her cape fluttered over to settle it on her shoulders.

I turned away and pushed up my nose, a Hevi-Hevian gesture of extreme confusion. I thought I knew what the *wakkam* was hinting at, yet it was hard for me to believe, much less say aloud. I turned back. "You don't really mean . . . " My words trailed off. I felt uncomfortable saying aloud what I thought she meant.

Wakkam Akkim smiled. "Rare is the *faelenga* that knows its own price, as the fisherfolk say on Skatwag Six."

As she walked past me to leave, the floor shuddered, as if we had been struck by an earthquake. But we were not on land, and the hook that holds us above the ground is designed to absorb such shock.

"What the heck was *that*?" cried the Grandfatherly One.

CHAPTER 10

[LINNSY]
MORE NEW ARRIVALS

"Linnsy, telephone!" called my mother. She was in the kitchen. I was in my room.

"Who is it?" I shouted.

"Misty!"

I groaned. Ever since I persuaded Misty to tell the truth about why Pleskit's Veeblax latched on to her in school, she seems to think we're best friends. We're not. All she wants to talk about is who likes who and junk like that, which I think is pretty boring most of the time.

This call wasn't boring. "So, girl," she said as soon as I picked up the phone, "when were you going to get around to telling me you've got a thing for Jordan?"

Too Many Aliens

My first thought when I heard this was: *I am going to kill that bigmouthed little worm, Tim.* Then I realized that the odds of Tim actually discussing something like this with Misty — who really does think Tim is a worm, at least socially speaking — were pretty low. Trying to be cautious, to not give anything away, I said, "What makes you think I like Jordan?"

Misty snorted. "Girl, when you drool in school over a guy . . . *I* know why."

"Skip the poetry. Am I really being that obvious?"

"You are to me. But not everyone has my fine eye for romance. So, you want me to call Jordan?"

"Why would I want you to do that?" I yelped.

"How else are you going to get things moving?" she asked, sounding as if it were the most obvious thing in the world.

"I don't want to 'get things moving,'" I said firmly, if not entirely truthfully. "Besides, I thought you were mad at Jordan for breaking up with your sister." I said this partly because I was confused, partly to buy some time to think.

"I was. But I had a fight with Cassandra this morning, so I'm even madder at her."

Before I could decide whether to have Misty call Jordan, my mother came to my door.

"Tim is here to see you," she whispered.

"Tell him to wait!" I snapped, then felt bad because my mother looked hurt, and none of this was her fault.

The thing was, it was hard to have a conversation with Misty about Jordan while Tim was in the apartment — partly because I didn't particularly want him knowing about my emotional life, partly because Jordan is always so rotten to him.

"Listen, Misty," I said. "I'll call you later."

"Whatever."

"And don't say anything to Jordan!"

I could almost hear her shrug over the phone. "I won't if you don't want me to. But, girl, if you don't stop drooling, somebody's gonna say something whether you like it or not!"

She hung up. I stared at the phone as if it were some slugbeast from another planet. With a sigh I put it down and went to talk to Tim, which — given the way our last conversation had ended — wasn't something I was exactly looking forward to.

He was slumped on the couch, looking like a guy

who's about to sing a country-and-western song telling how his dog died, his truck broke, and his wife dumped him for a lawyer. He had something strapped to his chest.

"Hi," I said, deciding to ignore the fact that he owed me an apology. I figured getting one out of him in his current condition would probably crush his spirit entirely.

"Hi."

I looked at him more closely. "How come you have the *oog-slama* strapped to your chest?"

"Bonding."

"Oh. Well, what's up?"

"Nothing."

I sighed. Clearly I was in for a round of boy-style communication. I couldn't even tell if this visit was about what had happened the last time he'd come up, or if there had been some new catastrophe in Tim World since we'd talked.

What I *could* tell was that he wasn't going to talk to me here in the living room where my mother might hear. But I didn't feel like inviting him to a conference in my room again. "Come on," I said. "Let's go for a walk."

He actually smiled for a second. "Sure. Let me get my coat."

***

It was snowing when we got outside — the kind of big, fat, fluffy flakes that make you want to catch them on your tongue. But there was no wind, and it wasn't all that cold, so it was fun weather to be out in.

We walked in silence until we got to the bridge we cross if we're heading for school. Standing in the center of it, we had a great view of the embassy hanging from its hook on the big hill in Thorncraft Park.

As usual, a crowd had gathered on top of the hill. The people stood at the edge of the barrier that keeps them from getting too close, staring up in wonder.

I thought again how cool it was that we had this thing that people were coming from all over the world to see right here in Syracuse. And how totally, utterly cool it was that I had actually been inside it.

Then I looked at Tim, who had been inside the embassy more than any other human. "All right," I said. "What's up? And this time I want an answer!"

Tim looked away from me. "I had a fight with Maktel," he said, twisting his hands in misery.

"I didn't know you'd even met him yet."

Too Many Aliens

"I went over to the embassy this morning," he said, still looking away.

I didn't say anything, just waited.

After a long silence Tim turned to face me again. Now his eyes were angry rather than miserable. "He was a real snot, Linnsy. And Pleskit didn't do anything to help!"

"What did you want Pleskit to do?" I asked, genuinely puzzled.

Tim's shoulders slumped. "I don't know. Just say something, I guess."

"He probably felt stuck in the middle," I said — not adding that, given the way Tim and Jordan felt about each other, I understood Pleskit's problem completely.

"Now I'm afraid they both hate me."

I shook my head. "Pleskit's too civilized for that."

"Yeah, everyone's civilized except me," he said bitterly. "Maybe I should go to Jordan to take lessons in how to be slick."

I flared. "What's that supposed to mean?"

I regretted the words immediately, since I knew very well what it was supposed to mean, and I didn't want Tim to answer the question.

I didn't have to worry about changing the subject. Tim grabbed my arm. *"Look!"* he cried, pointing to the embassy.

We stared in awe.

Plunging down from the sky was a beautiful silver-and-scarlet spaceship. It was heading straight for the embassy.

The crowd began to scream, racing back in panic. The ship looked for certain like it was going to crash. Then, at the last possible moment, it slowed to a near stop and moved gracefully into a position directly under the embassy.

Once it was centered, it floated up. When it hit the embassy, you could hear the *click* all the way from where we stood. Even more startling, the embassy, which is almost two hundred feet across the center, wiggled when it happened.

"Come on!" said Tim. "Let's go!"

He raced across the bridge and toward the embassy.

I took off after him.

At the end of the bridge we both came to a screeching halt.

CHAPTER 11

[TIM]
STRANGE WARNING

At the end of the bridge stood a tall man, one I hadn't noticed when we'd first stepped onto it. He held out his hands to stop us.

"Hold on," he said firmly. "Take it easy!"

"Did you see what just happened?" I cried. "I want to go take a look!"

The man shook his head. "Not a good idea."

"Why not?" asked Linnsy. She narrowed her eyes. "What are you, a Fed or something?"

The man shook his head, and his face shifted, changing from human to one covered with fur. "Not exactly," he said.

Linnsy and I began to back away.

Too Many Aliens

"I just came to offer a word to the wise," he said. "If you're smart, you'll watch out for Ellico *vec* Bur!"

Then he shimmered, and vanished.

I blinked. "Must have been a holograph."

"I don't care what it was!" said Linnsy. "Why the heck was he bothering us? And who's Ellico *vec* Bur?"

I glanced around, half expecting some other alien to shimmer into view. "He —they —are friends of Meenom's. Business partners, I guess. Come on, let's go down to the embassy. We should tell Pleskit about this."

But when we got to the park, the guard in the blue

dome I usually go through to get into the embassy wouldn't let us pass.

"Sorry, Tim," he said. "I know you're approved and everything. But you're not on the list for another visit today. And I can't get any answer from inside. I hope there's not a problem."

My guts were churning, from excitement, from fear, and now from upset at being shut out of the embassy. There was no reason to think it was Maktel's fault, but somehow I felt that if he hadn't been here, I would have been able to get in.

"Come on," I said to Linnsy. "Let's get back to the apartment. We'll see if we can contact Pleskit on my comm-device."

To my relief, it took only one buzz before Pleskit's face appeared in the round viewscreen. "Greetings, Tim," he said. He looked a little shaken.

"Greetings, Pleskit, and what the heck is going on over there?"

"Ah, you saw the arrival?"

"We sure did."

"We?" asked Pleskit. He bent his head so he could look past me. "Oh, hello, Linnsy."

She waved. "'Lo, Pleskit."

"The ship that arrived belongs to Ellico *vec* Bur. It turns out it was being repaired, and the Trader(s) had asked to have it delivered here when it was done."

"Well, they nearly scared the crowd outside the embassy into a mass heart attack," I said.

"Things inside the embassy were a little distressing as well," said Pleskit. "The Fatherly One was not properly notified, and he is less than amused. That's one reason I am in my room right now. Given his mood, I do not want to do anything to attract his attention. Maktel is here too."

"Hello, Maktel," I said, not entirely graciously.

"Greetings," replied a voice, coming from somewhere beyond Pleskit's face. He did not sound very gracious either.

"Listen," I said, "something else really weird just happened."

"I am not sure I am ready for more weirdness," said Pleskit. "I am on overload already."

"Yeah, I can tell," I said, reaching out to turn off the comm-device's smell transmitter. "But you'd better hear about this."

Then Linnsy and I described our encounter at the edge of the bridge.

"You're right," he said when I was done. "That is most disturbing. You are probably also correct that it was a holographic projection, which at least means there was not an unauthorized off-worlder here on the planet. But what was the purpose of their warning?"

"Obviously it was to confirm that Ellico *vec* Bur is not to be trusted," said Maktel, who had come to stand beside Pleskit.

"I'd agree," I said. "Except for one thing. The guy looked like he was the same species as Mikta-makta-mookta."

Pleskit gasped. Mikta-makta-mookta was our worst enemy. She had been with the embassy staff when they'd first arrived, but had turned out to be a traitor, one who had tried to suck every memory out of our brains.

"That complicates things greatly," said Maktel. "Just because the messenger was of the same species does not mean he cannot be trusted. On the other hand, it makes the message very suspect. So the question now is, can we trust the warning — or was it meant to cause some sort of mischief?"

But for that, none of us had an answer.

CHAPTER 12

[PLESKIT]
BRAINSTORM!

I wanted desperately to speak to the Fatherly
One, but he was locked away in conferences with
Ellico *vec* Bur for the rest of the weekend, and it was
late Sunday night before I finally had a chance to see
him alone. He looked weary and distressed — and even
more so after I told him what had happened to Tim.

"We have more enemies than I suspected, Pleskit,"
he said, his voice heavy. "Which may mean the oppor-
tunities here on Earth are greater than I realized. But
right now I am lost as to what is going on."

This did not make me rest any easier.

***

Bruce Coville

"Are you sure this school visit is a good idea?" asked Maktel at breakfast on Monday.

I glanced up from my *febril gnurxis*. "Don't you want to meet my class?"

I was surprised to realize that even though I had not always been entirely happy in this class, I had indeed come to think of it as mine, and I wanted Maktel to meet my friends and to like them too.

Of course, given what had happened with Tim, I had no guarantee that that would be the case. But I felt we had to try. I was even hoping that once we were in school, I might find some way to ease the tension between my two best friends.

A light snow was falling as we drove up the tunnel from the garage beneath the embassy, making the world look white and fresh. I thought Earth was especially pretty whenever this happened.

At school we had to go through the security clearances. "Yep, you're still you, Pleskit," said the guard once I'd been scanned. "And your friend here matches the profile the embassy sent for him."

Even McNally had to go through the check, to make sure he was truly himself.

Too Many Aliens

"This is horrifying," said Maktel as we walked down the hall. "What a violent planet this must be, that you require so much protection at your own school!"

"Actually, most of this equipment was installed because of problems we had with renegade off-worlders," I said, feeling oddly defensive of both the school and Earth.

"If you say so," said Maktel. But he didn't sound convinced, and I suspected he must have been thinking of other news stories he had seen while preparing for his journey.

Everyone in class seemed happy to see Maktel come through the door. Well, everyone except Jordan and Tim. It was probably the first time I had seen the two of them agree on anything.

Ms. Weintraub had placed an extra desk near mine on Friday so that Maktel would have a place to sit. Now everyone gathered around to meet him before class actually started. I realized with pleasure how different this was from my first day—how much more relaxed the kids were.

I could see Linnsy glancing back and forth from Maktel to Tim, who was standing at the edge of the group. I figured she must have heard from Tim how their first meeting had gone.

McNally stood a little way from us, but not leaning against the wall as he often does. I could tell he was hyperalert. It makes him nervous when too many people are near me. And, of course, now he was watching out for Maktel, too.

As we were talking, Maktel — forgetting the limited nature of human communication — made a particularly pungent fart to express a point.

"Whoa!" cried Jordan, waving his hand in front of his face. "How come there's never a Purple People Eater around when you need one?"

Naturally this caused Brad Kent, whom Tim refers to as "Jordan's Official Suck-Up," to laugh uproariously.

Encouraged by Brad's laughter, Jordan said, "Have you ever considered changing the name of your planet from Hevi-Hevi to Gassy-Gassy?"

"Jordan!" said Ms. Weintraub sharply. "*That* will be about enough!"

"You demonstrate a typical Earthling prejudice against anything or anyone who is different," I said to Jordan in exasperation.

He rolled his eyes. "You keep saying that, Plesk-o.

But face it—the main reason you're not really part of the class is that you keep yourself out of it. You live in that flying saucer and don't invite anyone in. So what do you expect?"

"Hey," said Tim. "He invites *me* in!"

Jordan sighed theatrically. "I was talking about human beings, dootbrain. You don't count."

Jordan's words angered me. Yet at the same time I was horrified to realize they held a grain of truth. Not about Tim; we had run a check on his DNA, and he really is human. But about my isolation.

Actually, I *didn't* realize this right away. But when Maktel and I were discussing the day on the way home, he asked, "Is it true what Jordan said?"

"About what?" I replied cautiously.

"That you have not invited anyone in your class besides Tim to the embassy?"

"Linnsy has been there," I said defensively.

McNally didn't say anything, but I could tell he thought this was pretty weak, since her visits had usually been the result of an emergency. What was worse was that I had to agree: it was a pretty feeble thing to say.

"Is there a reason you have not invited others?" persisted Maktel.

"I don't think the Fatherly One would like it."

"Have you asked him?"

I had to admit that I had not—which forced me to ask myself why this was so. Was it because my first few weeks had been so difficult? Or was I being overly shy? What kind of a diplomat would I make if that were the case?

I made the low and nasty fart of self-disgust. "What a *geezbo* I have been!"

I also made a decision: I would ask the Fatherly One if we could throw a party to welcome Maktel to Earth—a party to which we would invite my entire sixth-grade class!

It wasn't until that night, when I was preparing

for sleep, that I began to wonder if Maktel had raised the question of bringing other kids to the embassy because he thought it was a good idea — or as a way to bother Tim.

I shook my head in disgust. I was getting as suspicious as he was!

CHAPTER 13

[MAKTEL]
DEBATE

Pleskit's request for a party led to an embassy-wide debate. The Fatherly One—whom I still had not been able to see alone in order to pass on my secret message—called a staff meeting. We all assembled in the kitchen, which made Shhh-foop very happy. She slid around, warbling in ecstasy as she provided snacks for everyone.

The Queen of the Kitchen grew even happier when Pleskit explained his idea. Tentacles atwirl, she began planning a menu. "We can have *finnikle-pokta*," she sang, "and some *gerts* <happy fart> *skeedoop*. Do you think the children will like *febril gnurxis* if I form it into little cakes? Oh dear, oh dear, so much to consider."

She slid back to the counter to begin making notes.

"Shhh-foop, calm yourself," said Meenom firmly. "We have not yet decided whether this will happen."

Pleskit leaned to me and whispered, "Perhaps this idea was not as clever as I first thought. I am unsure how my classmates will respond to Shhh-foop's cooking."

Meenom turned to McNally. "What do you think of this idea?"

"Well, I hope you plan to bring in some extra security to keep track of all those kids," he replied. "I'm a bodyguard, not a babysitter or chaperone."

Ms. Buttsman leaped on the comment the way a *gnuck* leaps onto a *skakka*. "So, you're *opposed* to the party, Mr. McNally?"

McNally smiled. "Not at all, Ms. B., not at all. In fact, from a bodyguardly point of view, I think it's a good idea."

"You do?" asked Pleskit, sounding more surprised than was tactically wise.

"Sure," said McNally. "Having a party here will make the kids more comfortable with you. The better you fit in at school, the less the chance of some playground scuffle."

("Besides," he told us later, "I'm a party guy at heart!")

"Well, I still believe this to be a catastrophically bad idea," said Ms. Buttsman. "Not only that, it would be a serious misuse of embassy resources — resources that could be better spent cultivating the diplomatic mission."

"Ah," said *Wakkam* Akkim, waving her feathery eyebrows, "that objection does not take into account the importance of a balanced life. Work and play must both have their place, or a being does not thrive."

"Well, being as I'm dead, I've already put in enough work for one lifetime," said the Grandfatherly One, who had been placed in his portable transport device and brought to the kitchen for the meeting. "So my vote is, let's have the party! If you ask me, we should have had several by now. Kids, grown-ups, whatever. Besides, I'd like to see some of those kids from Pleskit's school again. Not that snot Jordan, of course. But most of the rest of them would be welcome here."

"I fear I cannot discriminate, O Venerated One," said Pleskit. "The class rule is that if I invite *most* of the students, I must invite all of them — including Jordan."

Too Many Aliens

The Grandfatherly One snorted through his speakers. "That's like saying if you have nine good *borznikki* on your plate and one rotten one, you can't eat the good ones unless you eat the rotten one, too."

"A *borznik* that has gone bad will never unrot," said *Wakkam* Akkim gently. "For an intelligent being, there is always hope for growth."

"Yeah, yeah, yeah," muttered the Grandfatherly One. "I think I need a nap." He pulled in his extensions and dropped the shutters on his vat.

I have known Pleskit's Grandfatherly One long enough to know that this action did not mean he was truly tired, just tired of the conversation. He once told me that the thing he liked best about being dead was that he didn't have to be as polite as when he was alive.

"Perhaps if we do have the party, there will be lots of leftovers," said Barvgis, patting his roundness happily. "I love leftovers!"

"I am afraid I must register a negative opinion," said Beezle Whompis, who had been flickering in and out of sight at the far end of the table.

I was surprised to hear this, since I knew that the Fatherly One's secretary had already helped Pleskit with some projects that were, shall we say, questionable.

"This is a professional judgment, younglings," he said, turning to us apologetically, "not a personal one."

"But I don't understand why," said Pleskit mournfully.

Beezle Whompis crackled out of sight for a moment, then reappeared. "The embassy is filled with sensitive equipment, much of which the Earthlings are not yet ready for. The potential for an embarrassing incident is fairly high. The potential for an actual disaster is present as well. While Tim and his parental unit have been very understanding about the mishaps that have already occurred, it is not likely that all the parents of Pleskit's classmates will be so easygoing. Should one of the Earth children stumble into an unfortunate situation, the repercussions could be . . . extensive."

"My point exactly!" crowed Ms. Buttsman.

Pleskit and I were even more surprised than Ms. Buttsman when Ellico *vec* Bur, who weren't staff members but had been invited as a matter of courtesy, entered the debate on our behalf. "We think such a party is probably one of the best things Meenom could do for his mission," said the Bur portion smoothly. "Remember, the Earthlings are approaching a season of holidays. Our studies tell us that they highly value such parties. Assuming all goes well, this could gather a good deal of favorable publicity for the embassy and its mission."

Then they reached over and pulled a *snergal* from behind Ms. Buttsman's ear. She looked startled, and did that very amusing trick some Earthlings have of turning bright pink.

Despite the conflict over the unauthorized landing of Ellico *vec* Bur's ship, Meenom seemed to think very highly of the Trader(s), and their opinion turned out to be the deciding one.

"We'll do it," said the ambassador, "and hope that our visiting friends are right. Now, if you'll forgive me, I have an appointment in Brazil."

I stood up. "Ambassador, if I could see you for a mo —"

I was cut off by Ellico *vec* Bur, who smoothly stepped in beside the ambassador and said, "We need to speak to you about a few details before you leave, Meenom. Now that our ship has arrived, we were thinking . . ."

That was the last I heard, because they were out of the room.

My suspicions about the Trader(s) doubled. It was clear—to me at least—that they were preventing me from being alone with the ambassador. Now I had another question: Why had they taken our side in the party debate? What were they hoping to *get* out of the situation?

A new idea twisted my *kirgiltum.* Was it possible that Ellico *vec* Bur supported the party for reasons exactly opposite to those they had stated? That is, were they secretly hoping it would be such a catastrophe that it would destroy Meenom's mission?

Or—and this thought was even *more* frightening—was it possible they were planning to *create* a catastrophe to do exactly that?

I would have been less apt to think this way if I had been able to deliver the Motherly One's message. But Ellico *vec* Bur's continual thwarting of my attempts to do so had sharpened my suspicions.

It was clear to me that Pleskit and his Fatherly One were entirely too trusting. Therefore, it was equally clear that it was up to me to keep an eye on Ellico *vec* Bur.

CHAPTER 14

[TIM]
ANOTHER MISTAKE

On Tuesday morning Pleskit raised his hand and said, "Ms. Weintraub, could I make an announcement?"

"Why, yes, I guess so," said Ms. Weintraub, looking a little startled.

I wondered what was going on—and felt hurt that I didn't know about it. Before Maktel got here, Pleskit would have consulted with me before making any kind of announcement to the whole class. I didn't even know what he was going to talk about, and I felt left out already.

Pleskit went to the front of the room and waited for

everyone to get quiet. Then he said, "Maktel and I have convinced the Fatherly One we should have a party at the embassy to celebrate the upcoming holidays. It will be on Friday night. You are all invited."

"*All* of us?" asked Jordan suspiciously.

"Every kid in this class is welcome," said Pleskit firmly.

The class started to applaud.

Jordan looked smug. Everyone else looked excited. Well, everyone except Misty. It didn't take me long to figure out that she was probably afraid that even though she was invited, she wouldn't really be welcome after the Veeblax incident.

I stole a glance at Linnsy to see what she thought of the party idea.

She didn't look back.

Then I looked at Ms. Weintraub and was startled to see that she looked deeply distressed.

The party was all anyone could talk about at recess, and I heard some wild guesses about what it might be like inside the embassy. The reason I heard these guesses was that I was drifting around the play-ground instead of hanging out with Pleskit and

Too Many Aliens

Maktel, which was what I really wanted to be doing.

I wondered if the cameras that the news media had permanently pointed at the schoolyard were filming me walking around, looking like a little lost dork. Finally I went over and leaned against a wall near where Pleskit and Maktel were talking to Chris Mellblom and Michael Wu.

McNally was nearby, leaning against the wall too, doing his best to look inconspicuous.

I tried to mimic his posture. He nodded to me.

I nodded back.

I would love to be as cool as McNally someday.

About the time I was getting up my courage to join Pleskit and the others, Linnsy walked up to the group.

I felt trapped. Facing all three of my social problems at once was more than I could cope with. But running away would make me look stupid. So I just pressed myself against the wall and tried to pretend I wasn't there.

It was a cold day, on account of it being December, but nice enough to be outside. Well, nice enough if you were used to it.

"I feel as if I've been sentenced to work in the northern wampfields," said Pleskit, huddling into his jacket.

"I take it that's like being sent to Siberia," said Linnsy. Then, her voice a little sharper, she added, "That's probably how Ms. Weintraub feels right now."

"What are you talking about?" asked Maktel.

Linnsy sighed. "Boys must be the same everywhere in the universe. Didn't you guys see the way Ms. Weintraub looked after Pleskit's announcement?"

"I did," I said, stepping toward them.

"How did she look?" asked Maktel.

"Upset."

"Upset and hurt," said Linnsy.

"Because we're having a party?" asked Pleskit, sounding confused.

"Because you're having a party and didn't invite *her*."

"I said everyone was welcome," he protested.

Linnsy shook her head. "What you said, precisely, was that every *kid* in the class was welcome."

"Why would Ms. Weintraub want to come to a kids' party anyway?" I asked, moving still closer. "She has to deal with us all day long. It would be like going to work again."

"Earth to Tim," said Linnsy, rapping me on the head with her knuckles. "Hello, this is your wake-up call! The party is going to be in the embassy, which is, like, only *the* place every human being on the planet would most like to get into. And now our entire class is going . . . except for Ms. Weintraub. You do the math, brainiac."

"Good grief," I muttered.

"Grief is correct," said Pleskit. His *sphen-gnut-ksher* was drooping, and I could tell he was moving into a major guilt episode. "Ms. Weintraub has always been good and kind to me. How could I have neglected to invite her?"

"Well, you're from another planet," I said. "Of course you're not going to get everything right here."

"Of course not," agreed Linnsy. "Look at Tim. He's lived here all his life without managing to develop social skills."

At first I was offended by this comment. Then I realized that this was the way Linnsy usually talked to me when we were actually getting along, so maybe it meant she had forgiven me for my outburst in her apartment. (Of course, that didn't mean I had forgiven *her* yet. But that was another matter.)

McNally usually stays out of the kid stuff, unless we ask him for help. So I was surprised when he walked over to us and said gruffly, "Look, why don't you guys leave this one to me? I think I can handle it without making it seem like you're suddenly taking pity on her."

"How?" asked Pleskit.

McNally smiled. "The McNally has his ways, Pleskit. The McNally has his ways."

"Your bodyguard is a very strange being," said Maktel, once he, Pleskit, and I were alone.

"Strange, but cool," I said.

"I would think everyone is cool when the weather is like this," said Maktel, sticking out his hand to catch a snowflake. Then he laughed. "Oh, you mean that *other* kind of *cool* you Earthlings are always going on about."

"Yeah, that kind," I said. "McNally definitely has it." I didn't add that McNally is pretty much my hero. But I was dying to know how he planned to solve the Weintraub problem.

A moment later Ms. Weintraub called for us to come in. So I didn't have time to figure out if Maktel and I were still fighting or not.

CHAPTER 15

[LINNSY]
PRE-PARTY PARTY

Wednesday afternoon my mother shouted into my room, "Call for you, Linnsy!"

I sighed and put down my copy of *The Hobbit*. When I came out into the hall, Mom whispered excitedly, "It's the alien boy! The one from your class."

I rolled my eyes. "For Pete's sake, Mom, he's got a name. It's 'Pleskit.'"

"Yes, dear," she said sweetly, holding out the phone.

I sighed. My mother has this ability to turn into a stone wall when I try to correct her behavior.

"Hey, Pleskit," I said, taking the phone into the closet. "'What's up?"

"'Up'? It's a preposition, indicating that something is in a skyward direction."

I sighed again. Sometimes it's hard to remember that, as brilliant as he is, Pleskit still doesn't have a complete grip on Earthly slang.

"No," I said patiently. "I mean . . . " I paused. What did "what's up?" mean, actually? "Uh, I just meant, 'What's happening?' You know, what's going on?"

Pleskit made a small sound of distress. "I know that," he said. "I was just making an attempt at humor. A failed attempt, I see. Anyway, I was calling to ask if you could help us with the party preparations. We are not entirely familiar with Earthly conventions for this sort of affair and could use some assistance."

"I'd be glad to! When do you want me to come over?"

"We're planning a pre-party party for Thursday night. I am also inviting Tim, in the hope that he and Maktel can settle some of their differences."

"What's the deal with them, anyway? Tim isn't a social wizard, but he can get along with anyone, except Jordan, of course. And if Maktel is your friend, he's got to be basically okay."

"I do not know," said Pleskit mournfully. "It's hard for me to understand how two people that I like so much can so dislike each other."

"I know what you mean," I said, thinking of Tim and Jordan — though I was a little startled to realize how much I really did like Tim.

"I should also tell you that the Fatherly One has suggested I ask Misty to come help."

"Misty! Why on Earth would you want to ask her after all the trouble she caused over the Veeblax last month?"

"In truth, that's the primary reason *for* inviting her," said Pleskit. "Please remember, the Fatherly One is a diplomat above all."

I stopped to think about that for a second. "Got it," I said. "It's not such a bad idea in terms of the party, either. Misty can be a pain in the butt, but she's really good at this kind of stuff."

Thursday afternoon Pleskit sent the embassy limo to pick up Misty and me at our houses, which was pretty cool.

Things were a little awkward when we first got to

the embassy, since Pleskit and Misty were still kind of wary of each other. It didn't help that Pleskit had the Veeblax on his shoulder when he greeted us. I just about had to peel Misty off the ceiling when she saw the thing. But then she calmed down and started playing with the Veeblax—which was actually all she had wanted to begin with—and pretty soon things were going along smoothly.

"Here," said Pleskit, passing the Veeblax to Misty. "You can hold it while I fetch the decorating materials."

Misty looked nervous but happy.

Tim came in a few minutes later, wearing that pouch with the *oog-slama* in it. He seemed startled to see Misty holding the Veeblax, but didn't say anything.

"Here we go!" called Pleskit. He and Maktel were coming down the corridor, each pulling a string attached to a floating pad that was piled high with what I assumed was stuff for the party. "This may be trickier than we thought," said Misty, looking at the piles. I nodded. I couldn't tell what any of it was.

"One of the main decorating devices for a Hevi-Hevian party is smell," said Pleskit, coming to a stop in front of us. He turned around and took a silvery tub off the floating cart. "This is an odor pot," he said, handing it to me. The tub fit comfortably into the palm of my hand. "We place them in strategic locations around the room."

"Uh, I dunno, Pleskit," said Misty as he handed her one of the tubs. "I'm not sure the kids will go for this." She looked at the little pot. "How do you turn this on, anyway?"

As she spoke, she twisted the top. Immediately a wave of odor flowed out.

"What a rapturous smell!" cried Pleskit.

Maktel started dancing in a dreamy kind of way.

Aliens. What are you gonna do?

"Smells like sardines to me," said Tim.

I nodded, pinching my nose as I did. I realized we had to talk Pleskit out of using the odor pots.

On the other hand, I loved the little light pots he brought out next. They were holographic projectors, and above them would be a vivid three-dimensional image — an image that kept shifting as time passed. Some of them shifted rapidly, some so slowly you couldn't see it as you watched, and would only notice it if you looked away and then turned back. The images were

mostly from Hevi-Hevi—famous. (according to Pleskit) buildings, strange and wonderful animals, and some beautiful plants. There were also some space scenes.

While we were working, Shhh-foop kept sliding in, singing worriedly about her food ideas.

She continued bringing in trays of food, most of which was truly weird, partly because a lot of it just wouldn't sit still.

"You can use the purple ones," said Misty decisively. "But the green things that keep whining have *got* to go."

I decided it was a good thing Misty and I were there. If it had just been the boys, they might well have let Shhh-foop spend the next day cooking a pile of goodies that would have driven the class into a mass barfing episode.

As soon as we finished discussing the snacks with Shhh-foop, we got into a big debate with Ms. Buttsman about what games would be appropriate. I don't know when the last time that woman saw a real kid was. I'm pretty sure she was never one herself. She wanted us to do the *most* baby things, like Pin the Tail on the Donkey.

Misty, on the other hand, wanted to play kissing games.

"Eeeuw!" cried Tim. "That's *disgusting*!"

"Not to mention forbidden," said Maktel.

I was glad, since this saved me from telling Misty I thought the idea was disgusting too — though when I thought about Jordan, I almost changed my mind. But I beat that thought down.

"We don't need games to have a good time," said Tim. "We all know each other. We can just hang out. The main thing is that people are going to want to see the embassy. Plus, Pleskit can bring out his stuff, which is so cool it will keep everyone busy for most of the night."

It was about the most sensible thing I had ever heard him say.

Later on he came over to me and said, "So, how do you think McNally is planning to solve the Weintraub problem?"

"I don't know," I said, deciding that, for the moment at least, I was speaking to him. "And I'm dying to find out."

Overall it was a really fun evening — except for one

extremely weird moment that occurred when Ellico *vec* Bur came in to see how we were doing. Though Tim had told me about the Trader(s), it took me a minute to get used to them. Even so, I thought they were pretty cool. But when Tim said, "Hey, is there any chance we could get a tour of your spaceship?" the look that crossed Ellico's face was frightening. It vanished almost immediately, replaced by a slick smile. "We're sorry," said the Bur part in its scratchy voice, "but that will not be possible."

They left the room almost immediately afterward.

Despite this, I thought the party was going to be fun and exciting.

As things turned out, it was more exciting than I could have imagined.

Not to mention life-threatening. Well, not just life-threatening. Considering the way everything worked out for me personally, I should probably say "life-changing."

CHAPTER 16

[MAKTEL]
SNOOPING

The decorating party was so stimulating that I had a hard time falling asleep, partly because of the excitement, partly because I had eaten too many *finnikle-pokta*, and partly because I was still disturbed by the tensions I felt with Tim.

To make things worse, Pleskit had invited his Earthling friend to spend the night with us, which had infuriated me. What could he have been thinking of?

At least I didn't have to share a bedroom with him.

But the most frustrating thing of all was the fact that I *still* had not been able to find a moment alone with Meenom to deliver the Motherly One's secret message. And now he had sent word that he would not be back until the night of the party.

I wondered how much it bothered Pleskit that his Fatherly One was away from the embassy so much. I think Pleskit must get really lonely for him sometimes.

While I was tossing and turning on my air mattress, tormented by thoughts of the Motherly One and home, of messages undelivered and Trader(s) not worth trusting, I heard a sound in the hall.

I was off the mattress immediately. Moving cautiously, I went to my door and opened a tiny viewport so I could look out.

Ellico *vec* Bur were walking down the hall, not moving with their usual confident stride but going slowly, stealthily, as if trying not to be heard.

Clearly this was something that needed to be investigated. No time to wake Pleskit or the loathsome Tim. I slipped into my robe, quickly turning off its lighting devices. Then I moved silently into the hall, where I pressed myself to the wall.

Following the Trader(s) was difficult because I had to stay far enough behind that they would not see me, yet remain close enough that I would not lose them — which meant staying just behind the curve of the corridor.

When they entered a tube and went up to another level of the embassy, I was afraid I had lost them. But the transporter returned to my level, and I was able to use the repeat button to get off at the same level the Trader(s) had.

But which direction to go now? The embassy's main corridor is a circle, of course, but there are spokes that run off it. And I certainly didn't want to start around the circle in the opposite direction from the Trader(s) and suddenly come face-to-face with them!

I enacted an old Hevi-Hevian choice ritual, performed by tweaking your *sphen-gnut-ksher* three times, then counting a rhyme off on your fingers.

Choice made, I headed to my right. At the second intersecting corridor I noticed a slight glow coming from one of the doors halfway to the outer window.

Again pressing myself to the wall, I inched silently down the hallway. As I drew closer to the open doorway, I dropped to the floor. Crawling forward, I peered around the frame. (I learned in Wilderness Way that you are less likely to be seen this way.)

Too Many Aliens

It was a comm-room. Ellico *vec* Bur were sitting at one of the transmitters, lit by the purple-blue glow of its screen.

"The situation is reaching crisis point," they said, speaking in Standard Galactic, which I had not heard since my arrival on Earth.

A longish pause followed while the Trader(s) waited for an answer. I could not hear it, because they had locked themselves into a secure connection. But the timing told me they were most likely speaking to someone in fairly close range, probably not more than a few million miles away.

"Of course," snapped Ellico *vec* Bur suddenly, in response to whatever answer had come in. "Now listen, if things develop as we fear they might, we'll need to make a speedy departure."

Pause to listen.

"Yes, yes, of course we've thought of that." Pause. "No, of course Meenom's not aware of what's at stake." Pause. "For now just continue to monitor the situation." Pause. "Right, right. Contact you tomorrow."

As they severed the connection, I slid back from the door and scrambled to my feet, hoping I could get down the hall and around the corner before they left the room.

I could not. Terror clutched my *clinkus* as I heard the Trader(s) enter the corridor. I wanted to run, but forced myself to hold still. Running away would not only be undignified; it would make me look even guiltier than I already did.

Besides, it would have been pointless, since the Trader(s) had already seen me. So I simply waved and made the salty-sweet smell of drowsiness. "You two couldn't sleep either, huh?" I said, trying to sound casual and friendly.

I could see from the look on Ellico *vec* Bur's faces that my ruse was not successful. Rather than say anything, the Ellico portion raised an eyebrow and half closed its other eye. His symbiote just glared at me with its tiny, beady eyes.

The implied skepticism pushed me into babble mode. "I think it was all those Earthlings we had here tonight," I said quickly. "I'm not used to that, you know. I tried and tried to sleep. Really! But I finally gave up and decided to go for a little walk."

"How odd," said Ellico *vec* Bur tartly. "We thought

Too Many Aliens

your Motherly One frequently gave parties that were attended by beings from all over the galaxy. We assumed you were more sophisticated than that, Maktel—sophisticated enough, in fact, to realize it can be unwise to listen to private conversations."

"I wasn't listening!" I cried, trying to keep my fear out of my voice.

The Ellico part of the Trader(s) raised its eyebrow again, needing no words at all to tell me how unbelievable they found this pronouncement. Then they swept past me, cape swirling and all four eyes blazing with anger.

I waited until they were out of sight, then bolted for the tube.

CHAPTER 17

[PLESKIT]
SUSPICIONS

"Pleskit. Pleskit, wake up!"

I blinked my eyes open. Maktel was standing next to my air mattress, dressed in his robe and looking upset.

The Veeblax, which had been sleeping beside me, eeped with alarm and transformed itself into the shape of a stone, something it does when it is frightened or startled.

"What do you want?" I asked groggily. "And what time is it?"

"I have no idea what time it is," said Maktel impatiently. "But Ellico *vec* Bur are up to something. I spied on them. They were sending a message. I didn't like the sound of it."

"What are you talking about?" I asked, struggling to pull myself to full wakefulness.

"Ellico *vec* Bur are up to something," he repeated, sounding as if he thought I was being stupid. "They just made a secure call out of the embassy."

"How do you know that?"

"Because I followed them!"

"Well, you're acting at least as suspicious as they are," I said. "What kind of *peevlik* follows people around in the middle of the night?"

"The kind who can't sleep and has reason to be suspicious," replied Maktel virtuously. "I'm sure those Trader(s) are traitors. You should have seen how angry they looked when they realized I'd been following them."

I waggled my *sphen-gnut-ksher*. "Of course they were angry! Wouldn't you be angry if someone was spying on you?"

"Of course! But that would be because I'm innocent!"

I laughed. "Then doesn't the fact that Ellico *vec* Bur got angry indicate that they're innocent too?"

Maktel looked furious. "All right, listen to this, Pleskit smarty-*orklit*. Before I left for Earth, my Motherly One gave me a message to bring to your Fatherly One. She said it was urgent, but she also said that it was important that I pass it to him in private. But Ellico *vec* Bur have managed to block every opportunity I have had to be alone with your Fatherly One. Don't you think that's suspicious?"

"It's just a coincidence," I said. But I don't think I sounded very convincing — mostly because all of a sudden I wasn't all that convinced myself. "Why didn't you tell me about this message?" I asked, feeling a little hurt.

"It was supposed to be a secret," said Maktel. He sounded more impatient than ever, which only made me more resistant to what he was saying.

Maktel noticed my hesitation. Farting decisively, he said, "All right, I'll show you. Where's your download box?"

I looked at him in surprise. Though we Hevi-Hevians can download a sensory memory from our *sphen-gnut-ksher* and then play it back so that we can re-experience it, it is very unusual to share a memory, since so many private thoughts and feelings will be attached to even the mildest events.

"I'm serious," said Maktel. "I must convince you that this is a dangerous situation."

I climbed off the mattress and went to get the download box.

Maktel used the box to download his memory of listening to Ellico *vec* Bur, then passed the box to me. I inserted my *sphen-gnut-ksher* and played back the memory. It was hard to focus on what was actually happening and shut out all the underlying thoughts that were simply echoes of Maktel's own fear and suspicion. One that I couldn't shut out, and that startled me, was his anger at Tim, and his unhappiness at what he thought was my betrayal of his friendship.

Concentrate! I told myself.

I did, and when I heard Ellico *vec* Bur speak and saw the look on their face as they swept past Maktel, I felt sick. This was serious after all.

"I apologize," I said. "This is very disturbing."

Maktel looked triumphant. Then he crouched beside me and whispered, "I think it's time we opened the Motherly One's message."

"That wouldn't be right!" I gasped.

"The embassy may be facing great danger," he said. "Danger that we need to be aware of. Your Fatherly One will not be back until the party tomorrow. That might be too late!"

It didn't take much more for him to convince me, which probably means I really wanted to open the message too. As soon as I agreed, Maktel went to his room to fetch the message.

While he was doing that, I went to wake Tim, who was sleeping in one of the guest rooms. Getting Tim had been a mistake as far as Maktel was concerned, as I could tell by the look on his face when he came back into my room. Though he did not say a word, his expression was clear: *Why did you bring him into this?*

My *smorgle* hurt. I wanted my friends to be friends. I most certainly did not want to have to act as a wall to keep them apart as if they were a pair of *quoink-zoopl*.

"Here it is," he said, holding up a package of *feebo beezbuds*.

My *kirgiltum* suddenly got very interested. I hadn't had any *feebo beezbuds* since leaving Hevi-Hevi.

Too Many Aliens

"Looks like a package of candy," said Tim, yawning and scratching his head.

"The message is inside," said Maktel scornfully.

Using his teeth, he cut a small opening in the corner of the package. Then he carefully pulled the sides apart.

He read the words on the inside of the wrapper, then blinked in astonishment and passed it to me.

CHAPTER 18

[TIM]
THE MESSAGE

I glanced over Pleskit's shoulder while he was looking at the message. I couldn't read it, of course, since it was in some alien language that was as hard to understand as my handwriting.

Pleskit's voice trembled as he translated it for me:

Dearest Meenom,

Something big is happening. I am not sure what it is, but I can tell you three things:

1. Earth is more important—and more valuable—than you realize.

2. You have more enemies than you realize.

3. Whatever this scheme is, Mikta-makta-mookta is mixed up in it.

Please be cautious.

Fondly,

Geebrit Ilkin

"I am disturbed by that 'fondly' part," said Maktel. "You do not think our parental units are interested in each other, do you?"

"Forget that!" said Pleskit sharply. "Mikta-makta-mookta is on the loose again. She could be up to anything!"

"Well, I told you this was serious," said Maktel, sounding a little as if he were talking to a three-year-old.

"What about the part that says 'Earth is more important than you realize'?" I asked, trying not to sound too eager. "What do you suppose it could mean?"

"I do not know," said Maktel. "It's hard to imagine, isn't it?"

"Don't start," warned Pleskit in a low voice, which I appreciated. He stared at the message for a while longer. "This is disturbing — terrifying, even.

But there is not much sense to be made of it. We will have to pass it on to the Fatherly One."

"But then he'll know we opened it!" wailed Maktel.

"You should have thought of that before you decided that was what we needed to do," said Pleskit sharply.

"Well, we won't need to worry about it until your Fatherly One gets back," I pointed out.

"Unless we should call to tell him."

"No," said Maktel firmly. "The Motherly One was very clear on that matter. No electronic message is secure. Any transmission we make can be captured and decoded. We have to give this to him in person. But what does it mean? And what does it have to do with Ellico *vec* Bur?"

"It doesn't necessarily have anything to do with them," said Pleskit. "The message certainly doesn't mention them."

"I suppose that could be true," said Maktel reluctantly. "But it's hard to believe. Why else would they be here?"

But for that we had no answer. And with Meenom out of the embassy, we couldn't think of anything we *should* do, which left all three of us jittery and sleep-less. We stayed in Pleskit's room, talking nervously, wondering what was going on, wishing desperately that Meenom would return to the embassy.

The amazing thing was, I almost started to like Maktel while we were doing this.

I stumbled through school the next day, and bombed a major science test because I was less than alert, and the part of my brain that *was* working was all tied up in thoughts about the Trader(s), about the message, about the party, about Pleskit and Maktel and Linnsy and Jordan. Maybe if we had had a little more rest, the three of us would have been thinking a little more clearly the next night, when it was time for the party.

Which could have made all the difference in the world — and for the world, I suppose, given the way things worked out.

Not just our world. The entire galaxy.

But that came later, of course.

CHAPTER 19

[LINNSY]
PARTY!

On Friday our class nearly drove Ms. Weintraub out of her mind, since all anyone could think about was the party at the embassy.

"We're just normal kids," said Chris Mellblom when we were out on the playground. "And we're going to a party at the alien embassy! My mother is so jealous, she wants to disguise herself as a kid and pretend she's my date."

"Eeeuw," said Larrabe Hicks. "That's sick!"

"I told her the same thing," said Chris.

By early afternoon Ms. Weintraub gave up trying to teach us anything and settled for just trying to keep us quiet.

Too Many Aliens

***

Misty and I went to the embassy early, since we were official helpers.

Pleskit met us as we came in. Tim and Maktel were standing beside him, Tim wearing that goofy *oog-slama* pouch. Pleskit looked tired and hassled. "Here," he said, handing each of us a purple card with a cord for putting around our necks. "These are your security passes. We're going to have a tour of the embassy later, but other than that, most of the rooms will be closed off. This will get you past security if you need to go to the kitchen to tell Shhh-foop we need more food or something."

He sounded as bad as he looked. "Is something wrong, Pleskit?"

His *sphen-gnut-ksher* drooped. "The Fatherly One called a couple of hours ago and said he would not be able to make it back in time for the party."

I felt really bad for him. I knew he had been counting on his Fatherly One being there.

I decided I would do all I could to try to make the party a success for him.

Ms. Buttsman came bustling in and asked Misty

and me to act as official greeters. This turned out to be a pretty good job, since it was fun to watch people as they came in, boggled by the trip up the tube, eyes popping when they saw the embassy for the first time, and popping even more when they met the staff. Several of them screamed the first time they saw Shhh-foop, and Larrabe nearly fainted when Beezle Whompis crackled into sight beside him without warning.

To my relief (I was feeling very responsible, since I was a helper) the class was (mostly) on its best behavior.

Not all of them, of course. Jordan and Brad spent most of their time standing at the food table, commenting on how weird the stuff was without actually trying any of it. When Shhh-foop slid in with another tray of food, their eyes bulged. Brad actually yelped and ducked behind Jordan.

"Silly Earthlings," sang Shhh-foop, sounding not in the least offended. "Have some *urkle-pidspoo*. It will make you smarter."

Jordan nodded. Brad stayed behind his back until Shhh-foop started back to the kitchen. Then he stepped out beside Jordan and the two of them started laughing.

Too Many Aliens

The two special security guards standing behind the table looked at them in disgust, and I realized that if I was going to make anything out of Jordan, the first thing I had to do was get him surgically detached from Brad.

Actually, the first thing I had to do tonight was get up the nerve to talk to him, which seemed stupid, since I talk to him all the time in school.

I noticed Rafaella Martinez sitting in front of one of the light pots, dreamily running her hand through the shifting images that hovered above it. When I went over to talk to her, she said, "Do you think Pleskit would sell me one of these? I'd love to have something like this in my bedroom!"

"I don't have the slightest idea. But I know he's big into trading. Maybe you can talk him into something. Look, there's Maktel. Let's go ask him."

I took her over to Maktel and explained her question. When I said, "Be back in a minute" and walked away, they both looked slightly alarmed. But I wanted to see what Jordan was up to.

Before I made it back to the snack table, I noticed that Larrabe was following Ms. Buttsman wherever she went. He seemed to think she was quite wonderful, which just shows how totally weird an Earthling can be.

I called Tim and Pleskit over. "Check out Larrabe," I said.

They watched for a few minutes, their eyes getting wider and wider. "I think he's got a crush on her," said Tim at last, which caused Pleskit and me to burst into giggles.

We were still standing together when McNally came in. Ms. Weintraub was with him, her arm linked with his. She had on a fancy dress, and more makeup than she ever wears in school. I was amazed at how pretty she was.

I grabbed Tim's shoulder. "Look!" I whispered. "I think they're on a date!"

"Holy mackerel!" he exclaimed. "Well, that explains how McNally solved the problem of inviting Ms. Weintraub, but . . . well, geez.'"

I knew what he meant.

There's nothing like your teacher arriving with an unexpected date to quiet down a party. The silence that fell over the room was deadly.

"Pleskit," I whispered urgently. "I think it's time to start the music!"

He hurried to the wall and farted a command. (I don't think I'll *ever* get used to that way of communicating, though Tim thinks it's hilarious.)

Immediately alien music began to play. At first everyone stayed quiet—stunned, I guess, by the weird beauty of the sounds. Then, slowly, the chatter began again—mostly people talking about the music—and the party came back to life.

"Good call, Linnsy," said Pleskit, who had come back to stand beside me.

"Get a load of Misty," said Tim.

I sighed. She was bustling around, doing her best "queen of the party" imitation, as if she were at the embassy all the time and the whole thing had actually been her idea.

"Don't you just want to slap her?" I said to Pleskit.

He looked startled. "We prefer not to use violence as a means for solving minor social problems," he said. "However, I agree that her presumption is annoying. Unfortunately, the Fatherly One wants me to be particularly nice to her, so I must be cautious about how much anger I display. Have you noticed Michael?"

"No, what about him?"

"He looks like he's in heaven," said Tim. "All this high-tech stuff is a total dream for him. Look—there he goes. I think he talked Beezle Whompis into giving him a tour or something."

"Perhaps he is a spy," said Maktel, who had managed to pry himself away from Rafaella.

"And perhaps you're a paranoid maniac," I said. It was a little rude. But then so was calling Michael a spy.

I decided I should go talk to someone else — namely Jordan, if I could get up the nerve. I drifted toward the snack table, where he and Brad were still hanging out. Then I stopped and turned away.

That made me angry with myself, so I turned back and headed toward them again.

By the time I had made three false starts, I was totally furious with myself. "If you want to be able to look yourself in the face tomorrow, stop being such a wuss!" I told myself firmly.

Taking a deep breath, I strolled over to the table. I started examining the snacks, as if I were actually interested in trying one — which, given the fact that my stomach was busy tying itself into a knot, was hardly the case.

Too Many Aliens

"Hey, Linnsy," said Jordan.

I looked up. "Oh, hi, Jordan!" I said, trying to sound surprised at seeing him. "How you doing?"

He shrugged. "Okay. This place is pretty cool, isn't it?"

I smiled. "Yeah."

He smiled back, which made my knees a little weak. Then he said, "But did you ever see such weird food? Looks like an explosion at the barf factory!"

That got Brad laughing so hard that he spewed punch through his nose, which was at least as disgusting as anything Shhh-foop had put on the table.

Jordan hooted with glee, and I decided that maybe he wasn't all that cute after all, at least not as long as he and Brad were so closely attached they might as well have been a symbiotic duad like Ellico *vec* Bur.

No sooner had this thought crossed my mind than the Trader(s) strolled in. They were dressed in an elegant gold-and-scarlet outfit. A pair of metal spikes rising from their shoulders held up their cape in a way that made me think of bat wings.

The Trader(s)' arrival created a nervous buzz in the room, and I realized we should have warned the kids about Ellico *vec* Bur. I shouldn't have worried. They sat

131

down and started to do some magic — little tricks with pieces of cloth and so on — and pretty soon several kids had gathered around them. Chris Mellblom was one of them of course, since he loves this kind of thing. He watched intently, then pleaded to be taught at least one of the tricks.

Ellico *vec* Bur smiled. "A master of manipulation does not share his secrets," said the Ellico portion softly.

"Not with outsiders," replied Chris conspiratorially as he took out a handkerchief. He rolled it up, stuffed it into his hand, and then with a flourish made it disappear — something we'd all seen him do a dozen times in school.

"I see I underestimated you," said Bur as Ellico raised an eyebrow. "All right, come with us."

Chris followed them out of the room.

Maktel was standing near me when they left. "I do not like this," he said nervously.

"What's the matter?" I asked.

"I do not trust Ellico *vec* Bur. Did you see how nice they were acting?"

I blinked in surprise. "You don't think Chris is in danger, do you?"

"I don't know," said Maktel grimly.

It was a weird situation. If I'd had any real reason to believe Chris was in danger, I would have rushed out to do something immediately. But this was just a suspicion from someone Pleskit had told me was notoriously suspicious of everything. How seriously should I take it?

I turned to ask Maktel another question, but he was gone.

CHAPTER 20

[PLESKIT]
FALSE ALARM

I was explaining the life cycle of the Veeblax to Rafaella when I noticed Maktel signaling to me. I was annoyed, because I had finally started to relax and have a good time. I tried to ignore him, but his signals grew more frantic.

"Excuse me," I said to Rafaella. "I'd better go see what Maktel wants."

"Catch you in a minute," she said. "Thanks for showing me the Veeblax—and for explaining how to eat those snacks. I don't like the purple ones that keep rolling around, but the rest of them are pretty good."

I hurried to Maktel, who was standing by the door. "What is it?"

"Ellico *vec* Bur are up to something. They just went off with Chris Mellblom."

I bent my *sphen-gnut-ksher* in a sign of skepticism. "Maktel, I agree that there is something very strange going on with the Trader(s). But you can't seriously think they would hurt one of my classmates."

"After what I heard last night, I don't know what to think, Pleskit. But they make me nervous. I believe we should follow them to make sure Chris is safe."

I knew Maktel when he was in one of these moods. It would be easier—and faster—to go along with him than to talk him out of it. "All right," I said. "Lead the way."

As I followed my paranoid pal out of the party room, I noticed he was making the fruity smell of satisfaction, which only added to my annoyance.

There was no sign of Ellico *vec* Bur and Chris, so we started walking to the right, which was the direction of the staff room. When we reached one of the transport tubes, we stopped to debate whether we should go up to Ellico *vec* Bur's quarters or continue toward the staff room. While we were discussing this, Tim caught up with us.

"What are you two up to?" he asked, panting for breath. He had one hand cupped over the *oog-slama* pouch, to keep it from bouncing while he ran, I supposed.

"We're checking on Ellico *vec* Bur," said Maktel. "I believe they are up to something bad."

"Man, you're brave," said Tim. "That guy . . . uh, those guys . . . scare me."

"You do not have to come," said Maktel sharply. "In fact, it would probably be better if you did not."

Tim glanced at me, which made me want to vanish. I did not want to be caught in yet another struggle between these two. "I'll be fine," he said firmly.

"Let's just go," I said quickly, then realized that that brought us back to the question we had been discussing when Tim walked up. "But where? We don't know where they've gone."

"I've got it!" said Maktel. "We should start by checking Ellico *vec* Bur's spaceship. Maybe we'll find some clue as to what they're up to." He paused, blinked, then said, "What if they're planning to kidnap Chris? We'd better hurry!"

I thought the idea that Ellico *vec* Bur wanted to

kidnap Chris was stupid. But the tiny possibility that it might be true scared me. After only a moment's consultation, Tim and I agreed with Maktel that we should start our search with the ship. This meant taking the transport tube down to the lowest level of the embassy, where we could enter the docking pod.

"This is great," whispered Tim as the door to the tube slid open. "I've been dying to get a look at Ellico *vec* Bur's ship ever since I saw it dock here."

The tubes are silent and fast, and we were at the bottom of the embassy in no time. I went to the control panel, but it took me a moment to remember how to open the docking pad. I was excited and nervous, terrified that Ellico *vec* Bur would catch us snooping, and even more terrified that Maktel's suspicions were correct and the Trader(s) were already here, about to blast off with Chris.

The silvery tube providing the entry to the ship lifted from the floor. Its door opened. Nervously Tim, Maktel, and I peered in. As we did, someone came up behind me and put a hand on my shoulder.

I cried out in fright and leaped into the air. This terrified the Veeblax, which tightened its grip on my neck.

"Oh, for Pete's sake, Pleskit," said Linnsy. "It's just me. What are you three up to, anyway?"

I was so close to *kleptra* that I could not answer. Maktel stepped in for me. "We're trying to prevent an interplanetary crime!" he said, his voice furious. "What are *you* doing here?"

Linnsy shrugged. "I needed to get away from the party for a while. Jordan was starting to annoy me."

Tim smiled. "That's a healthy reaction. Glad to hear you're coming to your senses."

Linnsy glared at him so fiercely that I wanted to fetch *Wakkam* Akkim to perform a peace ritual. "The other reason I came looking for you," she said coldly, "was because Maktel seemed so concerned about Chris. I just wanted to tell you he's fine. He came back into the party a few minutes after Tim left."

"Good," I said with relief. "We can go back now!"

"No!" said Maktel. "We should check the ship anyway. We might not get another chance, and I am sure Ellico *vec* Bur are up to no good."

"You were sure he was going to kidnap Chris too," I said.

"Maktel might be right," said Tim softly, which

139

surprised both Maktel and me. It also made me angry.

"Why do you say that?" I demanded.

Tim made one of those Earthling shrugs. "Look at all that's happened since you came here, Pleskit. I know you think things in the galaxy are all sweet and nice. But we've sure had a lot of people out to get us. I don't feel like we can trust anyone anymore. Add up what Maktel heard last night, the message his Motherly One sent, and how weird Ellico *vec* Bur acted when I asked about seeing this ship, and things sure seem suspicious to me. If Maktel thinks Ellico *vec* Bur are up to something, why not check it out?"

Maktel beamed in approval at this speech. I emitted the bitter smell of resignation. "All right. But we'd better do it fast. I don't want them to catch us!"

Slowly, moving as silently as we could, the four of us took the tube down into Ellico *vec* Bur's ship.

CHAPTER 21

[TIM]
TRUE ALARM!

I was more nervous about searching Ellico *vec* Bur's ship than I had expected to be.

"What are we looking for?" I asked, keeping my voice low.

"I don't know," muttered Maktel. "Something suspicious."

I figured he and Pleskit would have better luck spotting something than I would, since I couldn't tell what was suspicious and what was normal here. Heck, I couldn't even figure out how to open the doors until Pleskit showed me the right buttons to push.

The ship had four passenger cabins, plus one room

that was clearly for relaxation and exercise, though the machines it held were so weird, I couldn't begin to think how you would use them. While I was staring at the machines, Linnsy crossed to the other side of the corridor.

"What's this room for?" she called.

Pleskit, Maktel, and I went to join her.

"Storage space," said Pleskit. He poked his head in and looked around. "Nothing looks suspicious. We'll come back to it."

We made our way forward to the control room. I kept wanting to touch things, and drawing back for fear I would set off some sort of alarm. The *oog-slama*, dangling in the bag at my shoulder, began to wiggle, almost as if it were picking up on my nervousness.

The control room itself was beautiful, a sci-fi fan's dream — though, as in the exercise room, the equipment baffled me.

Not so Maktel. Clutching Pleskit's arm, he whispered, "This ship is not designed merely for going to a transit point. It can do time/space jumps!"

"Time/space jumps?" asked Linnsy.

"Most personal ships are designed just to carry you to an *urpelli*," said Pleskit.

Linnsy looked puzzled, and I quickly filled her in on what an *urpelli* is.

Pleskit picked up the explanation. "Standard pro-cedure once a ship this size reaches an *urpelli* is to load it onto a much larger ship, one designed to go back and forth through the *urpelli*."

Linnsy nodded in understanding. "Like a ferryboat."

Pleskit paused, as if searching his brain for the word, then said, "Exactly. And having a personal ship that can go through an *urpelli* is like having a car you can drive across an ocean! Ellico *vec* Bur must be either far more important or far richer than we realized."

"Or more dangerous," muttered Maktel darkly.

No sooner had he spoken those words than we heard a noise at the entrance to the ship.

"Someone's coming!" said Pleskit, his voice low and urgent.

"We've got to hide!" whispered Linnsy.

"This way!" hissed Maktel, scurrying back into the corridor.

We scrambled to join him in the little storage room that Linnsy had found. I was the last one in, and pushed the buttons to close the door behind us. It was dark

and crowded with all four of us in there. We pressed ourselves to the back wall, trying to find things to hide behind. I was flooded by deep terror. "What will we do if they find us?" I whispered.

"We'll say we were playing a party game," replied Maktel. "Now be quiet!"

Suddenly I felt a curious motion, just a slight stirring, so soft that it would have been easy to miss if I hadn't been so hyperalert at the moment.

Pleskit's eyes went wide. A terrible smell gushed from his *sphen-gnut-ksher*.

"What is it?" cried Linnsy. "What's happening?"

Maktel's *sphen-gnut-ksher* began to spark. "The engines! Ellico *vec* Bur have started the ship!"

"We've got to get out of here!" I cried.

"We can't let them know we're here!" said Maktel. "There's no telling what they might do if they realize we were spying on them."

"It's a little late to think of that now," I said.

I was relieved to see that Pleskit had already gone to the door. My relief vanished when he turned back toward us. Face twisted with terror, he said, "It's locked! It must lock automatically when the engines start."

"Help!" I shouted. *"Get us out of here!"*

"They can't hear you," said Maktel contemptuously. "The ship is —"

His words were cut off by a movement that made us all stagger.

"We're separating from the embassy!" cried Pleskit, his *sphen-gnut-ksher* emitting a shower of horrified sparks.

Maktel staggered to his feet. "It wasn't Chris that Ellico *vec* Bur wanted — it was us!"

Cold with terror, we stared at each other as Ellico *vec* Bur's ship picked up speed.

I heard Pleskit counting. "Thirty-seven," he whispered, "thirty-eight, thirty-nine." His shoulders slumped. "That's it," he said softly. "We've just left Earth."

I shivered in terror.

We had been snatched into space!

The story of what happened to Tim, Pleskit, Linnsy, and Maktel after Ellico *vec* Bur's ship blasted off will continue in Book 8:

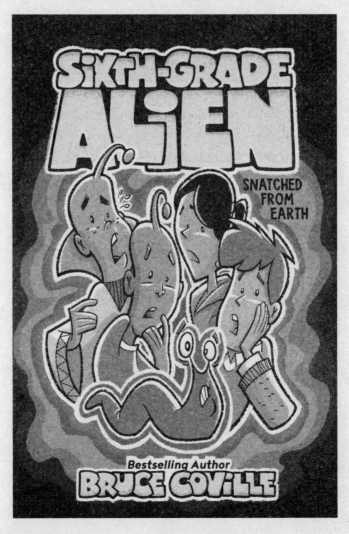

A GLOSSARY OF ALIEN TERMS

Following are definitions for the alien words and phrases appearing for the first time in this book. Definitions of extraterrestrial words used in earlier volumes of Sixth-Grade Alien can be found in the book where they were first used.

For most words, we are only giving the spelling. In actual usage many would, of course, be accompanied by smells and/or body sounds.

The number after a definition indicates the chapter where the word first appears.

BORZNIK (PLURAL: BORZNIKKI): A fruit grown on Ur-Borz-Ikl 5 and exported throughout the galaxy. Like all exported foods, it can be copied by replicators, or grown on any planet in reproduced conditions. But, as is also true of exotic foods, true gourmets say they can tell the difference. *Borznikki* are prized as much for their appearance — each ugly green fruit looks as if it has a face — as for their taste. True *borznikki* fans love to compete, with tales of the ugliest fruit they ever ate. (13)

FAELENGA: A kind of gemstone formed in the digestive system of the *akl-bing*, a ferocious water beast that roams the oceans of Skatwag Six. The stones actually annoy the beasts, which try desperately to cough them up. Divers brave enough to enter an *akl-bing*'s nest can make a fortune from a single stone. (Alas, these *faelenga* harvesters tend to have a very short life span.) (9)

FEEBO BEEZBUDS: Hevi-Hevian candy of extraordinary sweetness and caloric value; the recipe was first devised by Feebo Poylinga, legendary candy-maker to Glikksa the Fool. The sweet is widely considered to be the only good thing to come out of the tragic period when Glikksa ruled Hevi-Hevi with unprecedented (and never duplicated) stupidity. (2)

FUSHLOOB: A hopeless idiot. (9)

GEEZBO: (vulgar) A butt, or a hind end. (12)

GERTS <HAPPY FART> SKEEDOOP: A carbonated snack food that fizzes and bubbles in the mouth. A great favorite at children's parties on Hevi-Hevi, despite the persistent bit of folklore that warns of a boy who stuffed his mouth with these nuggets and died when his head exploded. (13)

GLORPTIOUS: An expression of delight having to do with how good it feels to squish mud through the toes of your bare feet. (5)

ORKLIT: Nonsense word used as an insult by children on Hevi-Hevi. (17)

PEEVLIK (PLURAL: PEEVLIKKI): A tiny animal found in the northern wampfields of Hevi-Hevi. Traveling at night, a *peevlik* will sneak into the nostril of a large beast—usually a *plonkus* or a *herklump*—where it may then live for the next several years. *Peevlikki* have become synonymous with "annoying sneaki-ness." (17)

QUOINK-ZOOPL: Small, hard-shelled creatures that have a fierce sense of territory. Their parental units separate the males, which usually come in sets of three, immediately after they hatch. If they are not separated, they will instantly begin to fight, and only one will be left alive by the end of the day. (17)

SNERGAL: A small green coin, often given to Hevi-Hevian children to mark a special occasion, such as their Hatching Day, or as a reward for learning a particularly difficult fart. (3)

TIGLOOP: A wormlike creature, two or three inches long, that likes to shelter in small holes, such as a nostril or an ear canal. If a *tigloop* enters a nostril already occupied by a *peevlik*, there will be a fight, which can be quite distressing to the owner of the nostril. (5)

URKLE-PIDSPOO: A high-protein snack made from ground-up fish heads. It is often claimed that the snack, which is quite spicy, will improve brain functioning. However, there is no actual proof that this is so. (19)

URPELLI: A warp in time/space that will propel any object that enters it a vast distance almost instantly. The analogy that teachers on Hevi-Hevi often use is that it is like having a door in your bedroom that opens onto another planet. This, however, does not take into account that any object not properly prepared and shielded for an *urpelli* jump will arrive at the other side in several million pieces. (2)

VEC: A term of relationship, signifying that two beings are linked in a permanent symbiotic union. Galactic scientists have cataloged over three hundred and fifty different kinds of *vec* relationships among intelligent beings. (3)

VECCIR (PLURAL: VECCIRI): The collective word for two or more beings merged in a symbiotic union. (3)

YEEBLE: An indeterminate pronoun, very useful when a speaker does not know if the thing *yeeble* is speaking of is a he, a she, an it, or any of the other seven generally recognized genders. The term is Standard Galactic, though it is also in common use in the local language of Hevi-Hevi. (2)